Emmaus

Jeremy Marshall

malcolm down

PUBLISHING

First published 2023 by Malcolm Down Publishing Ltd.
www.malcolmdown.co.uk

27 26 25 24 23 7 6 5 4 3 2 1

British Library Cataloguing in Publication Data.
A catalogue record for this book is available from the British Library.

ISBN 978-1-915046-67-3

Cover design by Jess Macaulay
Art direction by Sarah Grace

Printed in the UK

Chapter 1

Felix hacked away at the creeper blocking the gutter, but it was old, gnarled and wouldn't budge. In a cold fury, he took a swing at the plant but only succeeded in breaking the guttering. Frustrated, he threw his implement to the ground and went to find his supervisor.

'It's too old; the gutter's had it,' he said unrepentantly. 'I've tried to clear a path to fix it, but I've only managed to break it further.'

As he spoke, he couldn't help but see the irony in trying to escape from the torment of his own mind by volunteering for a charity based on the grounds of what was once Oakwood Psychiatric Hospital. The old Kent County Victorian buildings had been turned into upmarket flats. As part of the planning permission, a large area of gardens, cottages and greenhouses had been given to the charitable trust. Volunteers like Felix provided support for people with mental health challenges, many of whom had no gardens of their own.

He had stopped coming when his wife died three years ago, but his own struggles, insomnia and restlessness had prompted him, almost as a last resort, to offer his help again. Because of the strict Covid rules, they couldn't accept clients, but volunteers were welcome to keep everything ticking over.

So now here he was, and being back was agreeable. Nobody asked him where he had been for the last few years, let alone about Keziah, but plenty of them remembered him and offered a friendly greeting.

He took up the tools again and got back to work. As he was up the ladder, trying to repair the broken gutter and remove the leaves blocking everything, his old friend and sparring partner, Angus, came round the corner of the house.

'Well, I never.' Angus looked up at him in surprise. 'What the hell are you doing here, Felix? Where have you been?'

Felix, despite his anger, couldn't help but smile as he saw the startled man looking up. Angus was about his age, solidly built with a large brown beard.

'Angus, me old mate. You are also the last person I thought I'd see here. Last time we met, if you recall, you told me you'd had enough of us pesky Christian do-gooders for eternity and you were off to the pub.'

Angus laughed and was about to reply in kind with a few customary torpedoes at the ship of faith, but a lifetime as a lawyer had made him more observant than the average person. So, he paused and carefully observed Felix, who he thought looked awful. Grey, haggard and drawn.

Instead of more banter, he said, 'I remember that. I missed our verbal tennis matches with you trying to convert me. But how are you doing now? How's Keziah? You've changed.' By which he meant he'd aged.

Felix paused and looked around. He came slowly down the ladder. He thought he had heard voices, but they were alone. 'I've had a hard time. She,' he coughed and paused awkwardly, 'she . . . I mean Keziah, of course. She died.'

Angus's face fell. 'Oh, Felix, I'm so very sorry. I remember she was ill. How long ago was that?'

'Three years ago,' he said. 'Almost exactly. She died on Christmas Day, in fact.'

Over the years, he'd had to break the news to others several times. After a while, he'd found a way to temper the somberness, so he added, 'Just like Charlie Chaplin. It was the lung cancer she had years ago, if you recall. It came back and this time had metastasised. There was nothing anyone could do.'

Angus paused and looked to the ground. 'Yes, that's right. I suppose it must have been about three and a bit years ago that I stopped coming here. I got tired of all the paperwork you had to fill out. But then I came back about a year ago. I asked what had happened to you, but people just said you'd stopped coming. I'm so very glad our paths crossed again. Let's talk more over a pint – I'm so sorry for your loss. I really feel for you.' He reached out and touched him gently on the sleeve, then sighed and shrugged. 'We can't even do that though, I suppose, as the bloody pubs are shut. You will be glad to know I still have a thermos and my hip flask. Would you like me to help you first with that broken guttering and drainpipe?'

'Yes,' said Felix firmly, 'I'd like that very much. Thank you.'

So, the two men got to work. Felix explained what he'd done to the downpipe and proceeded to help Angus wrap some leading around it and secure it firmly in place. The guttering was choked with fallen leaves and twigs; here and there, joints had come apart and were leaking. The bottom of the drainpipe was completely blocked by a huge pile of dead leaves and moss and general rubbish – bits of paper, broken plastic, straw and goodness knows what else. The gutters were partly blocked, but the downpipe wouldn't work at all.

Eventually, Angus climbed back to the top of the ladder and forced the leaves down the pipe with a pole and Felix bent down and wrestled the debris out from the bottom.

Suddenly a large frog – or it could have been a toad, Felix was never sure of the difference – jumped out of the pipe. With that, there was a loud hiccup and gurgle and the water started to flow.

'We've just evicted a frog from his comfortable home,' laughed Felix.

Then something very strange happened. The frog hopped slowly away, but after a few yards it stopped, turned around, and stared fixedly at Felix. He looked firmly back at the frog, intrigued by its boldness. He could have sworn the frog winked at him. Twice. It almost seemed like it was trying to say something. Felix was curious.

With that, the frog turned again and hopped off purposefully into the beech hedge and disappeared.

'What's happening?' Angus called from up the ladder.

Felix didn't know what to say.

'All's fixed now, thanks,' he replied. 'Must have been a frog or a toad blocking it. Very strange frog, though.'

Angus was now down the ladder, wiping his hands free of leaf muck. 'A strange frog? What was strange about it, was it wearing earphones and breakdancing?'

Felix laughed. 'It must have had a bit of chameleon in it. It looked like it winked at me – twice – before heading off.'

'What exactly have you been smoking recently, Felix?'

This evoked a grin in Felix's strained features, and he found himself mellowing as they made their way to a spot in the garden which they both loved and recalled from previous visits. A path left the garden and fell down the steep southern scarp slope of the Downs. It then turned left, running along the crest before reaching the edge of the property marked by a barbed wire fence. From there, it turned southwards again and plunged steeply down into the woods.

The view from the bench next to the fence was downhill towards the south, and all that could be seen was a sea of trees, with the occasional green pasture island set into the ocean. Not a single house or building was visible, and the trees were naked, spared of their leaves in the winter chill. Each season bought a new vista and, in a few months, their fresh green clothing would be breathtaking.

There was, Felix felt, something grand but awfully sad about the bare trees, and he said so to Angus, who was pouring coffee from the thermos.

'Ah, the pathetic fallacy,' said Angus.

'The what?' Felix bent his eyebrows.

'It's when you attribute nonexistent feelings to nature. The waves sobbed on the beach.' Angus grinned at him, offering him the full thermos lid. 'You must know that. Didn't they teach you anything at your school?'

Felix grinned. He took the coffee, declining the offer of a wee dram. He cupped his hands around the thermos top and leaned forward.

'It's strange we should meet again. I always enjoyed our debates. I could deploy my best arguments and bowl you my favourite googlies. I don't think I ever shifted you an inch, mind you.'

'You are welcome to try again,' replied Angus.

'Sadly not. To be honest, Angus, I'm struggling big time with everything in my life now. I just don't understand how a loving God could allow all these terrible things to happen to me. The pain and the grief I'm feeling are simply too much. I feel I've given my life to him, and now I get this back? Why did these things happen to me? And now I don't know what to do. Once Keziah died, I decided eventually to take early retirement, and this is my last few months as a vicar. I'm glad I did leave, because my heart just isn't in it anymore. I'm saying things I don't really believe. It's not that I've become one of your motley crew,' he smiled at Angus, who surprisingly was listening intently,

'but I'm no longer in my own crew either. I'm like someone shipwrecked in the ocean and just drifting around on a few logs.'

There was a long silence. Then Angus sat back, resting his arms on the back of the bench.

'Thank you for telling me all that. I can't argue with someone who's been shipwrecked.'

The two men shared a small smile.

'Can I ask you one question, though?' Angus leaned towards him. 'How do you feel towards your God? Do you think he doesn't exist, or does exist but doesn't care, or does exist but is hiding?'

Felix stared into the distance. He didn't know the answer.

Chapter 2

'To be honest, Angus,' Felix finally managed, 'I guess more than anything I feel angry with him, even at times on fire with rage. I feel like saying "Look, I dedicated my life to serving you, and this is what I get?" Keziah dying, of all days, on Christmas Day. What an absolute joke. Is his aim to humiliate me? Am I an object of heavenly amusement? And when I ask him about it, I don't even seem to get any reply, nothing at all. I ask my questions, but an answer never comes. So, I feel completely stuck. I don't know what to do or what to think. Sure, I'm retiring, but then what? Play golf for the rest of my life?' He halted very abruptly, almost retching in frustration.

Angus both scratched and shook his head. 'I'm sorry, and to be truthful, I don't know what to say either. I feel a bit sad – don't laugh – when I hear you talk like that. Who am I going to argue with now? Can't play argument tennis if my partner has lost his racket. Seriously though, my friend, I could see what a difference your faith made to you: you loved it, and it gave you meaning. Even if it was a bit delusional, and yes, it was also your job and yes, I can see now it must be tough to be stuck in limbo. What do you think you might do?'

Felix thought for a while. He could taste the coffee grounds in the back of his mouth.

'Well, to be honest with you, and I appreciate you listening,' Felix grunted in amusement. 'And even being almost sympathetic. In fact, you want to be careful that it doesn't catch on.'

Angus snorted. 'Don't worry, no danger of that.'

'One good thing is, I'm financially in good shape. Between us, I had a tidy nest egg from when I stopped working in the city and I've done very well with it. In fact – I don't know whether to laugh or cry – since Keziah died, I've spent a lot of my spare time playing the markets and I've done very well. When Covid struck, I waited until the market tanked, and then in April, I bought all the stuff that had collapsed like airlines and hotels, plus Bitcoin and Dogecoin and silver, and a few other funky bits and pieces. I haven't sold much yet, but I'm sitting nicely. Don't need to ever work again, to be frank. I like that feeling of security. But that, of course, still leaves me with the question of what to do.' His voice trailed off as he wondered if he'd said too much.

'How about you, Angus?' Felix sighed, turning his head. 'What's happened to you?'

'Well, business is booming. There's always a demand for divorce lawyers and the beautiful combination of Christmas and Covid will mean my phones will be ringing off the hook in January. I've made more money than I know what to do with. But I'm not really that happy. I keep thinking, "Is this it?" I've reached the top of the ladder and there isn't anything there. If you'd offered me at 21 all the money and houses I have now, including the gorgeous farmhouse in Southern France that I can't even visit, then I'd have snapped your hand off, but now I've got them all I'm still . . .' He paused, trying to place the word. 'Restless, I guess. Then of course, the irony of being one of the UK's leading family law experts and having just divorced my third wife doesn't escape me. And my children – most of them are angry with me in one form or another and I don't even blame them. I'd love to talk to them, really talk to them, and Christmas reminds me of that more than anything else. Funnily enough, volunteering at this place is the one thing I truly enjoy. I can clearly see the difference we make to the people we are trying to help. I can't say the same thing about my legal work, to be honest.'

Felix patted him lightly on the shoulder. 'Now it's my turn to be sorry, old friend. We are just a couple of tired, beaten-up hopeless old crocks.'

Angus stood up. He didn't know what to say and talking about his kids had left a lump in his throat. 'Let's walk on,' he said, packing up the thermos and having a final swig from the hip flask.

The path now plunged downwards through the trees towards the pool, skilfully cut into the forest, halfway down the slope. Alongside the path, the water ran down steeply and noisily through its channel.

Although Felix has been this way before, he'd never looked at the sign by the pool. He stopped to read how the marvel of Victorian engineering worked.

Angus laughed as he saw Felix puzzling over the sign.

'There we see a typical arts graduate. You need a scientific background, my dear fellow. The principle is simple: you use a lot of water coming down the hill,' he pointed back up the channel, 'to drive a little water back up the hill to the reservoir by the house, which then supplies the whole estate. Two thousand gallons a day, so you can water your blessed gardens. The Victorians knew their stuff. And it still works today."

Felix smiled again despite himself. Angus was a bit of a rogue: he'd had a few run-ins with the Kent Constabulary about his driving and his alcohol intake, which Angus delighted in regaling his friends about. He had three marriages and various other affairs; he was a convinced atheist. By rights, they should have been opposites and wholly at odds. Yet Felix was fascinated by him and his roguish antics.

The pool was completely still and, apart from a few dead leaves drifting on the top, there was no movement or sign of life. Felix felt suddenly odd, like the pool was waiting for someone or something. He looked around but there was nothing to see. Everything was as it should be. Impulsively, he threw a stone into the middle of the pond, but other than the ripples gently lapping the stone edges, nothing happened. However, on the far side of the pool, his attention was caught by a glimpse of something red.

'Let's go round. I want to look at something,' he told Angus.

When they got to the opposite side, near to where the water came down, there was a row of ancient holly trees between the pool and the water on a little strip of grass. They must have been planted when the pool was built, and it looked as if they had been well cared for, as the ground around them was neatly tended. All the trees were naked of any fruit except for one, which was covered from head to toe in bright red berries.

'That's strange,' said Felix, looking at Angus. 'Why does one tree have so many berries and all the others have none? And how come the birds haven't eaten any?'

Angus shook his head. 'I'm a scientist and lawyer by training, not a gardener. I haven't a clue.'

Felix looked around for a gardener, as if expecting one to be at hand, but could see no one. Then, once again, he felt, or heard, or could sense a strange tremor of expectancy. It was as if someone was saying something which he couldn't quite hear. But there was no sign of anyone or anything. The woods were silently snoozing in their winter slumber.

The two men climbed slowly back up the slope as the path wound through the trees. Here and there, they glimpsed the land away to the south, rolling gently like the bumps and hollows of an untidily made bed. Felix knew that if this were spring or summer, they'd be passing people constantly, but in the current frost, all was quiet.

Back at the house, Felix started packing away his tools, his mind returning to the strange frog. It was nowhere to be found.

'What are you doing for Christmas Day?' Angus's voice came abruptly.

Felix paused, before saying, 'I was going to join up with two of my sisters, but now with the regulations changing I can't go, so I guess I will be on my own.'

Angus jumped straight in as he helped Felix tidy his tools away.

'Look,' he said, 'I'm on my own too. My latest lover, not Abbie, the one after her – her name's Francesca – well, she and I had a big argument last week, about Covid funnily enough, and she's gone back to her place in London. I'm "Tom all alone." Why don't we each make a Christmas picnic and go up on the Downs behind your place? Even the irritating village Gestapo Covid agents can't object to that!'

Felix hesitated. He was going to decline but then again, he really enjoyed Angus's company. He didn't want to ask anyone for help, but after all, Angus had offered it, hadn't he? He hadn't asked Angus and it would seem ungracious and rude to decline.

Angus could sense Felix's hesitation. 'Of course, if you've got a better offer elsewhere . . . Don't let me derail you from your hundreds of party invitations.'

Felix laughed. 'No, I have no alternatives whatsoever, don't worry. Angus, I'd like that very much and I can't tell you how much good it's done me to meet you again, thank you.'

Angus looked almost embarrassed. They parted, agreeing to meet at Felix's on Christmas morning at ten o'clock, each armed with a picnic.

As he drove home, Felix was troubled. The winking frog and the berry-covered tree made him think. Someone was trying to say something to him, but he simply couldn't understand the message. Was it God speaking? He thought briefly, but then in almost the same instant dismissed the idea as absurd. Why would God use a frog? Was there even a God anyway?

Chapter 3

The next morning was Christmas Eve, and Felix woke up early after a fitful sleep and decided to go for a walk. His house was just behind the ancient church, which was supposedly dating back to Anglo-Saxon times. This was very convenient when he was working, but slightly awkward now that he had stepped down as vicar but hadn't actually left the vicarage yet.

His successor had not yet been announced and, although Kemsing was a large village, it may be that there was no successor at all, and it would become one of several churches sharing a vicar. He hoped not, but the Church of England was struggling. His last ever diocesan meeting – on Zoom, of course – had been full of gloom over falling congregations and dwindling finances. A management consultant bought in by the Archdeacon had talked dismally of 'economies of scale' and 'limiting factors'.

He felt he was getting out at the right time, especially because he, in any case, was so riddled with doubts. But he absolutely didn't want his old friends in the parish to know that; it wouldn't be fair for his doubts to infect or discourage them. Covid had given him the perfect excuse to shut up the church and try to avoid his congregation. Sometimes, of course, he couldn't avoid them, and he had been friendly as they chatted, but had tried to stay guarded.

'How are you doing, vicar?' they would say.

'Oh, I'm fine,' he always replied. He loved the word 'fine' – such a safe word.

His Archdeacon had persuaded him to use a counsellor after his wife's death, and the word had become a running joke between him and his therapist.

'Fine again this week?' asked Stefan with a smile at the start of every session.

'Fine as always,' Felix would reply.

This morning he felt so restless again that he had to escape the feeling of being imprisoned. Without a clear plan, he slipped out and used a narrow alley that took him away from the church and the village, towards the recreation ground. They had a dog called Max, which he and Keziah used to walk there every morning and evening, but the old dog had seemed to fade away after Keziah's death. It was more her dog than his anyway, and he didn't want another one. He quite enjoyed the freedom to come and go as he wished, not being tied to any church services or appointments.

The recreation ground sloped steeply down from north to south. There was little through traffic in Kemsing, although you could hear the hum of the M26. To the north were trees clothing the Downs left and right, except immediately above the village, where the Green Hill was bare. When it was snowing, the village children absolutely adored it, as it was the most terrifyingly brilliant toboggan ride ever, though people had to make sure they didn't stay on too long and crash into or even through the fence at the bottom.

There was movement ahead, catching his eye. Someone was working on the cricket pitch, sitting on a large ride-on mower. As he neared, he saw it was Guy, the captain.

'Hoping for some Christmas cricket?' Felix joked.

Guy paused the roller and jumped off. He was a large jolly man and a deadly slow bowler.

Opposing batsmen's eyes lit up when he came on, but Guy knew how to make the ball dip and turn. What Guy needed was two trustworthy fielders at long off and long on to catch the attempted sixes. When Felix played – whenever they were short – he always hid at square leg. That and the third man were the safest positions for an old crock like him.

'Hello Felix,' said Guy. 'Good to see you mate, long time no see. How are you doing?'

'I'm fine, thanks,' he said, 'but you may need a new last reserve as I'm moving on in a couple of months.'

'Where are you going? Be sorry to lose you. Do you remember the last game you played against Bidborough? What a match.'

Felix remembered it well. They had been short of players one day in the last summer before Covid, so not only had he played but he'd even been promoted to number seven. A dizzying height, given he was normally a confirmed tail-ender. They'd needed over one hundred runs when he came in and after him were just the kids – thirteen and fourteen-year-olds, keen as mustard, but unlikely to make many runs. When he was on seven, he'd chipped an easy chance to extra cover but inexplicably the fielder had spilt it. That was the chance he needed.

With ever-growing confidence, he'd kept scoring – only singles and twos, as he couldn't hit boundaries except down the steep slope to the south. And at the other end, the teenagers had suddenly become hopeful, and their belief spurred them to hit the ball powerfully. Although a couple of them had got caught out, Felix had kept the team together.

'Keep it steady, boys,' he'd said to the lads. 'We can do this.' Meanwhile, the opposition, who had been sure of victory, started to get rattled; a few hilarious misfields with the ball shooting through the wicketkeeper's legs only made the captain more irritated.

With amazingly only twenty more runs needed for victory and the last batsman in, the dynamic changed. They had nothing to lose, but now the seesaw switched. Before that moment, Felix had been enjoying himself, but now he suddenly felt pressure both to win the match and to reach what would have been his first-ever fifty. A fifty! He'd hardly even been in double figures before. Bidborough put on their fastest bowler and Felix knew it was now or never.

The last batsman was in – not a teenager, but Old Bob at the other end. Bob was the reserve's reserve: he could bowl, but he couldn't bat to save his life. It was Felix or nothing, and after a few swipes, somehow they needed eight to win. He hated fast bowling and, trying as he did, he couldn't avoid closing his eyes. In pounded the bowler. Felix closed his eyes and prodded at the ball. He was so late in the shot, as everyone said afterwards in the pavilion, that it was laughable. The ball hurtled past him but was so fast it also beat the wicketkeeper and raced away for four byes. Fuming, the visiting captain moved the fine leg round finer to avoid a repeat.

Four to win. Four for his fifty as well. Singles were no use, as Bob certainly wouldn't last a ball.

But how on earth was he going to get a four? In came the bowler, gathering pace up to the wicket, and he bowled. This time, Felix took an almighty swish but instead of a satisfying thud there was a nasty snick. The ball hit the inside edge of the bat. Somehow, by a coat of varnish, it avoided the leg stump and raced away. As everyone held their breath, the fielder behind the wicketkeeper raced around the boundary, heading for the exact spot where he had stood for the previous ball. He threw himself at the ball, which glanced off his despairing outstretched hand and trickled over the boundary. The match was won.

Felix remembered collapsing to his knees in relief. What a feeling.

'Yes, it was the match of my life, Guy. Well, maybe if I don't move too far I could still play, I guess.'

'You've always got a welcome here, mate. Are you set up for tomorrow ok? A few of us might go for a walk and then "accidentally" meet at the pavilion in the afternoon for a quick beer. You'd be most welcome. We'd love to see you.'

Felix appreciated his friendly invite but didn't want to fully commit.

'Yes, maybe I'll try,' he replied. 'Thank you for all you do for the club, Guy. We couldn't do it without you.'

Guy climbed back on the roller. 'Happy Christmas!'

After his walk, Felix went back to the house but again felt terribly restless. The house felt full of ghosts – not only Keziah, but also her mother who had lived with them some years ago. If a room wasn't reminding him of Keziah, then it was her mother. He'd got on well with her, for they had a shared interest in chess. Pretty much every evening they'd play a game, and they were very evenly matched. Keziah had no interest in chess but loved watching her two loved ones battling it out.

It was an extremely old house, full of sloping floors and corners which often weren't quite at ninety degrees. Felix would miss its idiosyncrasies and quirks, but he couldn't stay there. He hadn't even begun to think about where to go next. Covid didn't exactly make it any easier. London would be an obvious choice, but the last time he was there it felt like a ghost town. Ideally, he would have just packed everything away and travelled the world until the restlessness was out of his system. The thought of going no further than Cornwall or Northumberland didn't fill him with joy.

He had until 31st March to leave the house, so that was enough time. Maybe Covid would be over by then. He could go to places he had always wanted to see, like India or Chile.

In the afternoon, the restlessness still persisted. He wondered if he should go and see where he had scattered Keziah's ashes. Maybe he could find some peace there. There was none to be found at home.

Chapter 4

As he had lunch, the words of a carol Keziah liked kept playing round and round in his mind like a stuck record. 'Trace We the Babe.' But try as he might, he couldn't make sense of it. 'Trace' sounded like drawing round something to make a copy. But that made no sense. Or did it mean 'track'? But how, he thought, how am I to track someone who's been dead for two thousand years? He had to correct himself, realising that as a vicar, he should probably think of Jesus as alive, not dead. In addition, of all things to be told to track, a baby was the least likely instruction to work, as by definition a baby couldn't move. He wasn't getting anywhere. Time to get out. He felt like a trapped tiger in a cage.

It was Christmas Eve afternoon, so where should he go? Lots of places would be shut because of Covid or because of Christmas Eve itself. A thought had come to his mind before lunch and the more he thought about it, the more he liked it: go to one of Keziah's favourite places and the place where he had scattered her ashes.

Since they had met at university, she had adored trees. He smiled to himself as he recalled their first date and her indignation as a biologist that he didn't even know the difference between coniferous and broadleaf trees. She had delighted thereafter in teasing him about his inability to recognise even the most obvious of tree species.

'What's this then, Mr Blockhead?' She would quiz him with a broad smile on her face.

Sometimes he would in turn get great pleasure in winding her up by pretending an oak was an ash or vice versa.

She had injected not just knowledge but enthusiasm into his cynicism.

When they had moved to Kemsing for his first proper job as a vicar, Keziah had thrown herself into the fight against the destruction of many trees just a few miles away. The M25 orbital motorway around London was nearly finished, and the last missing link was between Sevenoaks and Swanley, only a few miles to the north. The published route would have taken the motorway right through the 'Valley of Vision', where Samuel Palmer and William Blake had dreamed their strange dreams, mixing English pastoral with biblical visions. Hundreds of ancient trees, some of them painted by Palmer himself – oak, hornbeam and yew – would have been ripped up. Keziah had threatened to chain herself to one of the trees in Lullingstone Park. This hadn't made his job any easier, as many of his parishioners thought the M25 was an excellent idea and would be good for property prices.

'Was that your wife I saw on BBC Southeast, waving a placard?' Several people asked him after one particularly stormy protest at the public inquiry.

Felix had demurred and tried to change the subject, but one of them was insistent.

'I'm sure it was her, because I recognised that red duffle coat.'

Felix had felt embarrassed and later had tried to steer his wife into calmer waters.

'By all means protest, but do you have to be at the front with such a large placard?'

She bridled at his clumsy efforts to deflect her. 'Don't talk to me about what your stupid parishioners think. You should be ashamed of yourself. Who cares what others think? Do the right thing and don't be such a coward.'

She returned five minutes later to deliver a second salvo. 'Oh, and by the way, aren't we supposed to be the stewards of the earth? It doesn't belong to us, but to God. I'm sure some vicar or other once said that in a sermon. Or was it just a load of BS?'

Eventually, thanks to the campaigners' efforts, the motorway has been shifted a few miles further north, thus saving Palmer's beloved valley. Although, as Keziah pointed out, it thereby ruined a different swathe of the North Downs.

When she had been taken ill, there was nowhere she had enjoyed visiting more than Hucking. The area had come to her attention through the Woodland Trust, of which they were both members.

'Look at this,' she said to Felix one morning over breakfast, near the start of her cancer treatment.

She thrust a leaflet on top of his bowl of Shreddies, entitled 'The Man Who Hated Trees'. Felix read it as he munched through his cereal. It was about a farmer just a few miles away to the east on the Downs who had systematically denuded his land of all trees. What had triggered this deranged behaviour was very hard to say: possibly lengthy disputes with the local authorities about planning and tree preservation orders. Finally, he had died and the land, being chalk downland, was of little agricultural value. The Woodland Trust was asking for money to buy several hundred acres and, over time, plant it with trees.

Felix continued to finish his Shreddies. Keziah simply wasn't going to be stopped.

'Come on, you old Scrooge,' she said, poking him in the ribs with a wooden spoon that was conveniently to hand. 'All that money you've made from wheeling and dealing in your portfolio. Finally, this is the chance to do something good with it.'

Felix demurred. 'I'm not such a huge fan of trees, like yourself. Maybe the farmer was just being efficient?' This wasn't how he truly felt, and Keziah knew it. Seizing the spoon firmly by the handle, she lightly tapped him on the head with it.

'Let's knock some sense into you,' she said, hands returning to her hips. 'Firstly, you always say, "All that I have is yours and vice versa." As the money is mine, I want to give some – and not a derisory pittance, but something we will notice. Something that costs. And secondly, Ebenezer, think of the tax break you will get – just the other day you were boasting about it when you donated to your old college, which God knows doesn't need the money. Forty-five per cent, wasn't it? Come on, don't be a skinflint.' And with that, she gave him a slightly harder but still playful tap on the head with the spoon.

Felix realised he needed a tactical retreat. Keziah could up the physical ratchet playfully.

'I'll tell you what, let's go and see it. Look, there's an open day in a couple of weeks,' he said, pointing to the leaflet.

Keziah snorted like a war horse. 'Very well. But don't think you're going to make me forget or change my mind – because I won't.'

Sure enough, two weeks later they had turned up on a beautiful May morning at the pub car park in Hucking. Even though they were early, the park was full, and they had to pull up on a nearby grass verge. What Felix noted, with amusement, was how socially mixed the group was – you could tell that by their cars. Gleaming new Range Rovers stood cheek by jowl with battered old Land Rovers splashed with caked mud. Ancient Morris Minors with faded 'Atomic power? No thanks' stickers in their rear windows were boxed in by sleek new Audis.

Two people addressed the crowd once they had gathered. One was a stylishly dressed lady with bobbed hair who introduced herself as Sue; the other looked like, and turned out to be, a genuine 'forester' called John. He looked like he'd spent his whole life outdoors, with jolly red cheeks and nose, battered hat, and a well-worn Barbour jacket.

The large group rambled uphill with the golden May sun streaming down their backs. To the south and east, the land fell away, and in the far distance, the traffic crawled like metallic beetles along the M20. That was the only sign of human interference, for ahead there was just bare chalk downland liberally sprinkled with weeds as the land had been left fallow since it had been offered for sale.

John identified one of the weeds as not a weed at all but a rare monkey orchid, and soon Felix and Keziah, who knew nothing about orchids, were together with a few others, hunting for more. It actually turned out to be fun. A lady with a severe haircut and a pair of dungarees looked as if she should be on a CND March; she had a guide to the orchids of the North Downs and was engaged in a vigorous but friendly discussion with an elderly gentleman about whether a specimen was a Lady Orchid or the wonderfully named Duke of Burgundy. John had to be summoned to break the tiebreak and as he did so, he pointed out to Felix that he was nearly standing on a Butterfly Orchid – hard to recognise, as it wasn't in flower yet.

It had been a golden day. The sun streamed down, lighting up the land, and the people bonded, animated by the rightness of their cause. Old and young, right and left, rich and poor, all felt a love swelling in their hearts for this wee bit of land and a desire to put things right.

On the way back to the car, Sue explained to John and Keziah what they wanted to do: buy as much land as they could, plant some trees and let nature take its course.

Back in the car, Felix squeezed Keziah's knee and looked at her lovingly. 'Darling, I give up and now I get it. How much?'

She gazed back at him, her eyes lighting up in a familiar way as she smiled.

'Thank you. I love you. You can decide.'

This wasn't at all what he was expecting. He knew he had made a lot of money trading cryptocurrencies. Millions. Keziah had no idea of how much money they had, as she never bothered to ask, not least as up until then she had never asked to spend any.

'We can afford £100,000,' he said after a while.

She replied in surprise, 'Wow. That's lovely, thank you so much.'

Immediately after he said it, a feeling of guilt worked its way into his heart. He realized he was taking advantage of her trust. He hadn't told her an outright lie, but he had deliberately and callously deceived her. He should have pledged much more, but he couldn't, and he didn't know why. So, he had deceived her. And the weight of that had stuck in his mind ever since. He had made the pledge, but he couldn't shake the thought that had she known their true position, she would have wanted to give much more.

Chapter 5

As he retraced the drive to Hucking, he recalled two other visits.

One was another golden day: this time towards the end of September, a few years after the first visit but just months before Keziah died. She had changed for the worse and he couldn't help but continually notice her deterioration, although silently. All her hair had fallen out, though she hid it skillfully under a colourful headscarf. Below, her face had a grey pallor, as if all the colour had been washed out of a painting. Her breathing was laboured and she found it difficult to climb the hill, having to use Felix as a sort of tug in order to tow her up the slope.

As she climbed, she kept coughing with a gasping and rasping sound.

This time, perhaps fortunately, they were on their own. They climbed again to the spot where Felix had nearly stood on the rare orchid – a mishap she reminded him of, both laughing and coughing as she did.

'Some friend of nature you are, you clumsy old goat – wiping out Kent's rarest orchids!'

He smiled back at her. Having carefully checked the ground for orchids, rare or not, they sat down. This time, while the far view of the valley and the motorway was the same, the nearer slopes were utterly transformed. Where a few years ago there had been nothing but bare chalk downland, today there was an explosion of young trees in all directions. Some of the trees were nearly as tall as Felix, and their leaves waved backwards and forward in the wind, beginning to turn golden and brown.

Suddenly, with no warning, she said, 'When I'm gone, leave me here.'

Felix blanched and blurted out, 'What do you mean?'

She laid a hand on his shoulder, a mist in her eyes. 'This is what I mean: when I'm dead, I'd like you to scatter my ashes here.'

Felix became even more agitated and stood up and looked down at her.

'Please, Keziah, don't say that. You are not going to die. God, I'm sure, will heal you: I've prayed and prayed and prayed and I just know he will. So don't say something like that, please don't.'

She smiled back up at him. 'Look, Felix, I admire your faith, but I'm sorry, I think I've had it. If your God can do something, that's fine, but in my bones, I think this is it.'

Felix didn't know what to say, for the phrase 'your God' was a tough one to swallow. All their relationship he'd had the stronger faith, while Keziah often struggled, especially with the church, its strange politics, and its odd and quarrelsome people.

'What do you mean, "your God"?' he asked hesitantly.

She looked ahead into the far distance. 'Look, the God you've been telling me for years will heal me hasn't shown up. Maybe God doesn't even exist. Strangely enough, I think now more than ever that God does exist, but a different God to the one you described, and in fact, I'm waiting for him to show up. Even more strangely, I'm expecting him, sort of looking forward to him coming. But he's a different kind of God. He's coming on his terms, not ours, and that's just the way he is.'

Felix didn't know what to say. He felt a wave of doubt sweep over him, like a fog bank enveloping a headland. He had simply changed the subject and they had spent the rest of the time happy enough, marvelling at the way the trees had grown, bursting out of their tiny tubes, creating havens for wildlife. Overhead, a buzzard circled slowly, almost lazily, watching intently for its prey. Was God a sort of buzzard? Felix wondered. Seeing everything from on high, watching and seeing but only descending occasionally purely to eliminate us?

He had been sure that God would heal her, a certainty strengthened by friends who had sent him texts and messages encouraging him to think that way. How could God, he argued to himself, not help him, given that he had abandoned his career in the city in order to serve God? He devoted his life not to his love of making money and doing deals, but to the mundane and, at times, the tedious weekly round of services with his elderly parishioners.

It wasn't fair.

Most of his life he'd been slaving away and never really asked God for anything, and yet now the one time he had done so, the request seemed to have been denied, or better put, ignored. Even a denial would be better than nothing. He became angrier and angrier. God wasn't fair.

In the car on the way home, he had wanted to ask her more about what she had meant but couldn't. He'd felt afraid he would ask a question to which he wouldn't like the answer.

Suddenly, again, without any warning, she said to him, 'You're upset with me about what I said earlier, aren't you?'

He was taken aback. How did she know what he was thinking?

'Yes, I suppose I am,' Felix admitted. 'God seems very far away. Why doesn't he answer me? Why does he hide or look down on me but not do something?'

She spoke softly. 'Wait. Hold on. Let more time go by. Millie said something to me the other day. She said, "If there is a God, then even though he seems to be hiding, eventually he will show up."'

Now Felix was even more surprised. Millie was Keziah's older sister who, when they met, had clicked instantly with Felix because they were both trying to convince the sceptical Keziah. Millie was devoted to her church, volunteering in every conceivable ministry: children, young people, homeless people, and refugees.

Unfortunately, though, there had recently been a terrible scandal in her church. Her vicar, whom she had worshipped for years, had been arrested and imprisoned for possessing a huge store of child pornography. His demise had been all over the newspapers. To make it worse, some of the people in the church had stood by him, saying it was the devil's work to bring him down and that he had been convicted unfairly. As a result, Millie completely lost her faith and broken all ties with the church.

'Millie?' asked Felix in surprise. 'I thought now she didn't believe in God, she hated church?'

Keziah pursed her lips. 'She's more open than you might think. Isn't it strange that after all these years she's now a bit like me? We are both not waiting for Godot but waiting for God.'

Felix snorted at her joke. 'Well as I recall, the whole point of that boring-as-hell play is that Godot doesn't ever turn up. Maybe if you are right, it's more apposite than you know.'

Keziah just smiled again. 'Oh no, I'm sure he will turn up, but maybe not when and how you expect.'

Felix fixed his eyes on the road. He realised that they were at the point of crossing over: she, who was always somewhat the sceptic, was going towards God, while he, the religious man, was moving away. He didn't want to move that way, but he felt he couldn't help himself: he was sliding downhill and couldn't find a place for his feet to hold.

The next time he had been at Hucking, it was just him, his three sisters, Millie and Keziah's mother. This time it was spring, but still bitterly cold and the wind tore through the leafless saplings. Their little group had climbed, him carrying Keziah's ashes, up to the spot where they had sat only six months earlier. He had wanted to say something before they scattered them out – something from the Bible, or anything at all – but the words just wouldn't come. The others knew he was struggling with everything and was thinking of leaving the church, so they simply smiled kindly at him. He appreciated their love and compassion, for despite himself, it warmed his cold heart.

'Let us all say something suitable,' said Keziah's mother. 'It's too much for you alone to carry; let us share your load.'

He had mumbled his thanks and then there was silence. His cold hands gripped the container.

Then, to his surprise and amazement, Millie, of all people, proclaimed in a clear and powerful voice:

'The Lord is my shepherd; I shall not want. He maketh me to lie down in green pastures: he leadeth me beside the still waters. He restoreth my soul: he leadeth me in the paths of righteousness for his name's sake. Yea, though I walk through the valley of the shadow of death, I will fear no evil: for thou art with me; thy rod and thy staff they comfort me. Thou preparest a table before me in the presence of mine enemies: thou anointest my head with oil; my cup runneth over. Surely goodness and mercy shall follow me all the days of my life: and I will dwell in the house of the Lord forever.'

Then she repeated with great emphasis and strength of feeling, 'You will dwell in the house of the Lord forever.'

The others all said 'Amen' in chorus. Felix just couldn't. He opened his mouth, but nothing came out. Then he lifted the lid from the container and wordlessly cast the ashes into the air, where they hung for the briefest of seconds until the wind scattered them, and then they were gone.

Chapter 6

In the car, alone, on the way back home after the ashes were scattered, Felix felt guilty. Firstly, for being unable to say anything a few minutes earlier. He had wanted to say something, but nothing would come. It was like trying to be sick and only retching noises coming out. The beauty of the words Millie had recited and the simple way she had said them struck him with power.

'Walking through the valley of the shadow of death' was exactly where he felt he was, but he couldn't feel the presence of God.

He felt and he feared rather, he had to admit, evil: the evil of cancer, which had imperceptibly spread through his wife's body at a frightening rate. Like a wildfire that was deadly quiet and overwhelming. He recalled the oncologist's face, kind but sad as he reviewed the latest results.

'I'm sorry, but the treatment doesn't seem to be working. The tumours have grown and there seem to be a couple of new sites. I'm so sorry.'

Keziah had taken the news on the chin, but Felix felt angry, and the feeling had never left him. Not only had God not answered his prayers – which was embarrassing as well as sad, with all the people he'd told with conviction that Keziah would be healed – but now God seemed to be hiding. Then the thought entered his mind: maybe there just was no God, nothing to hide, nothing to find. He had decided as he drove home that he would have to resign as vicar once a suitable opportunity came up. He couldn't encourage belief in someone whom he wasn't sure even existed.

But strangely, the deeper guilt was not the loss of faith but his gift of money to the Woodland Trust. He felt he had shortchanged his wife, who had trusted him. He had to admit that if he was honest with himself, he had deceived Keziah about the original gift.

Now he had the perfect opportunity to make it right. Give a donation in line with what she would have wanted. He knew he should do it, but he just couldn't. He loved the security of the balance in his account. Whatever else happened, he was safe. It felt like a 'get out of jail free' card. When he was growing up, he had no money at all and there was an illicit thrill as his balance kept climbing. So although he repeatedly felt he should do something, in the end, he had done nothing and tried to put it from his mind.

Now, as he was driving back to Hucking on Christmas Eve afternoon, the thought recurred with great power. It was as if someone, maybe Keziah, was sitting next to him in the empty passenger seat and poking him.

'Make it right, you miserable old Scrooge.' He could almost hear her saying as she poked him in the ribs.

'Do the right thing.'

Strangely enough, as Keziah's health had got worse, his investments had got better. He liked the comfort and certainty of tracking the markets and he enjoyed competing with a group of his old mates from the city. He enjoyed their company in their WhatsApp group with all its banter and comradeship.

His shares recently had been doing well yet again, and he could rib his mates who had sold their EasyJet and technology shares earlier in the year while he had doubled down. They retorted, claiming that he had only done this with divine assistance, which was unfair. He hadn't the heart to tell them he didn't believe in divine assistance anymore.

The debate in his head about the gift was becoming more insistent as he parked in the near-empty pub car park and started walking up the hill. It was strange he would feel so bad about that and yet only feel numbness about leaving his faith and his job. He wanted to make the additional gift, but he had a feeling of powerlessness to do it.

At the top, he paused again at the place where they had scattered her ashes. She, who was once so living and vibrant, was now gone. Utterly gone. Surely that couldn't just be it? He accepted death as inevitable, but not such a young death. Either, he thought sadly, there was no God at all, or there was one, but he was a capricious God swooping on one person whilst sparing another.

From some long-forgotten corner of his mind came a Bible verse: 'I cry out to you God, but you do not answer. I stand before you, but you don't even look.'

That was good; he liked that, the verse helped. It was honest and just how he felt. Who said that? He couldn't remember. Perhaps the psalmist or Job? Or was it someone like Augustine?

'Oh God,' he prayed, 'if you exist, answer me. Or at least look at me.'

He looked around, expecting something amazing to happen, but the only noise was the wind in the leaves.

He went on, the hill sloping gently to the south and the feeble winter sun providing some little warmth on his face as it began to go down in the west. He looked at his watch. In half an hour or so it would get dark, and it would be time to go home. The thought was depressing. He had planned to meet up with two of his sisters for Christmas lunch, but the government's sudden announcement a couple of days ago meant his and everyone else's Christmas was cancelled. It was a form of purgatory – always winter but never Christmas.

At least he had the chance to go for a walk with Angus. That was a fine chance to meet him again at the gardening centre. He craved real human company, not the half-life of Zoom. Continuing his way downhill, he found his steps drew down towards an old drover's trail. He remembered Sue from the Woodland Trust telling him that these ways were very old, probably pre-Saxon, made for the ancient Jutes to drive their swine to market. For countless generations, pigs had gone through this road to be fattened up for slaughter. No doubt these Jutes had their happiness and sorrows, their births and deaths, but who knew or cared for them now?

As he descended the path, the banks of the trail grew steeper, and the trees grew thicker overhead. It was like being in a tunnel. He was suddenly very conscious of being all alone. Everything was still, breathless. He at once became conscious of the same sense of waiting and anticipation he had felt yesterday, but this time it was something much stronger. It almost became overwhelming.

He realised the feeling was like homesickness, like the longing for his long-vanished holidays of childhood when it had taken all day to drive to Cornwall. Before the motorways were built, it had the feeling of an odyssey. The sun began to go down in the west, and then finally, before you saw it, you could smell the sea. Rounding a bend, there it was, the long-expected ocean, so exciting and inviting. You had come to your home. The door of the cottage on the clifftop stood open in welcome, and the light streamed out of the home into the gathering dusk.

He remembered Millie's husband Si, who was Welsh, telling him that there was no English equivalent of the Welsh word 'hiraeth', which meant homesickness for a home to which you cannot return. A home which maybe never was, a sense of grief for the lost places of your past. It was, said Si, something far deeper than mere nostalgia. That was what he felt now.

As he struggled to make sense of his feelings, a wind began to blow almost playfully through the leaves which filled the floor of the tunnel, tossing leaves here and there, twisting them up like little helicopters before gently landing a few feet down the trail. The wind kept moving and swirling, next playing around his trousers, flicking his calves, then rising and ruffling his hair.

Felix stopped walking and turned right round to look intently back up the slope. By now it was very dark, and the last setting rays of the westering sun cast a final dying gleam on the dancing leaves. Round and round they went, rising and falling, fanned by this little breeze.

They seemed, like the frog and the berry tree, to be trying to send him a message.

He felt afraid, but it wasn't a fear like when you're watching a horror film. It was rather like when he was once on the dock at Southampton when an aircraft carrier was arriving. The carrier docked and simply dwarfed everything else, all the other boats and people, making it all laughably insignificant.

After a few minutes, the wind seemed to shift and head on down the trail, and he realised that his time was up, and he must get back to his Zoom calls. Reluctantly, he began to climb back up the path.

Was that God? Had that been some kind of message? That's when he remembered, he had only asked God for an answer a few minutes ago. So maybe this was some kind of reply? But what could he make of leaves being blown carelessly here and there, illuminated by the last rays of sunlight? What kind of an answer was that?

He came out into the open and yet again passed the place where they had scattered her ashes. This time, as he passed by, he recalled Millie's words and he finally decided.

It was time to do the right thing. He couldn't live with the way he'd deceived his wife.

Chapter 7

Back at home, it was now wholly dark. The faint shape of the yew trees at the end of the garden could just about be seen. Felix got up and drew the curtains. He sat back in his chair in the study, thinking about what to do with his money. Whether to give that gift or not. He just couldn't decide.

He looked up and, of course, he was surrounded by theological books. Once they had been his friends, helping him with his work, but for the last few years they had been silent and abandoned as he wrestled with his grief and loneliness.

He looked out the window at the gathering darkness. Maybe he should try reading one again? He had always loved a writer called JC Ryle, so at random, he picked one of his books and started to flip casually through the pages. A passage caught his eye.

'How tenderly Christ speaks of the death of believers. "Our friend Lazarus sleeps," says the Lord. Lazarus is the friend of Jesus even when he is dead. We can boldly say: "I will lay me down in peace and sleep for you Lord alone, make me dwell in safety."'

He thought about Keziah's last hours. The few words from Ryle seemed to speak to him. He remembered sitting by her bed in soulful agony, but strangely, the more his anguish increased, the more she seemed to be at peace. She was drifting in and out of consciousness. Once or twice, she smiled weakly at him. Her breath came more and more slowly. Whereas a few hours before she had been breathing with difficulty and in pain, now she looked more like a child falling asleep. Gently he had touched her hair, regrown after the chemotherapy, even though what was once golden and abundant was now sparse and grey.

Her breathing came with gaps now. The nurse had come and placed her hand on his arm.

'It won't be long now, I'm sorry,' she said.

Felix tried to say to himself one last despairing prayer for God to step in and save her. A few minutes later, he realised she hadn't breathed for a while. The nurse came over and again put her hand on his arm.

'She's passed,' she said.

Now, as he sat in his study, his mind couldn't stay still; it was like a caged animal pacing up and down. How attractive Jesus was as a person. How he would have loved to have been there and heard him teach. How kindly and compassionately he had dealt with Lazarus's grieving family. Something in the words he'd read struck him with raw power. He especially loved the words: 'I will lay me down to sleep in peace.'

That was what Keziah had looked like – not unlike a child going to sleep in its bed with its parents at hand. Where was that from? He googled it and found out it was Psalm 4:

'Answer me when I call to you,
my righteous God.
Give me relief from my distress;
have mercy on me and hear my prayer.
How long will you people turn my glory into shame?
How long will you love delusions and seek false gods?
Know that the Lord has set apart his faithful servant
for himself; the Lord hears when I call to him.
Tremble and do not sin;
when you are on your beds,
search your hearts and be silent.
Offer the sacrifices of the righteous
and trust in the Lord.
Many, Lord, are asking, "Who will bring us prosperity?"
Let the light of your face shine on us.
Fill my heart with joy
when their grain and new wine abound.
In peace I will lie down and sleep,
for you alone, Lord,
make me dwell in safety.'

'Answer me,' Felix thought desperately. God had answered the two sisters' prayers and their brother had come back to life. What it would have been to be there.

But, on the other hand, he was torn, for that was then and this was now: what use was a comforting story from two thousand years ago? Maybe the story wasn't even true? Maybe it was reassuring in the same way a fairy story with a happy ending gives warmth to a small child afraid of monsters. What had Richard Dawkins said? 'Christianity is a fairy

story for those afraid of the dark.' What if that was true? He had been wasting his time on an illusion.

He was certainly afraid of the dark: it was dark in his study, apart from the light cast by the overhead lamp directly into his lap. The mood of the nation was dark, as dark as he could ever recall. Covid reared up like a gigantic black hand. Darkness hung over the nation, and the room and his heart both felt darker than he could ever recall. Death was waiting, and then oblivion.

'Was the story actually true?' he mumbled under his breath, realising that this was his central dilemma.

Once he had believed it was so, and had, in fact, dedicated his life to convincing others that it was too. After Keziah's death, he became convinced to the contrary – that it probably wasn't true – and kicked himself for wasting his life on a fairy story. Now, especially after what had happened in the last few days, he wasn't sure what to think. The feeling of longing and waiting and the strange frog and the fertile tree and the spiral of wind-blown leaves were each explicable in their own way, and utterly trivial really, but together they seemed to be trying to say something. He couldn't tell what.

He realised he wanted the gospel story to be true more than anything, but couldn't find a way to make it true.

Again, a deep feeling of anguish and longing washed over him.

'Oh, God,' he almost shouted out loud, 'if you are real, please speak to me, tell me who you are, don't leave me in the dark with no light.'

There was silence.

Then suddenly, yet again another image came into his mind: Michael Caine. Strange. What had God got to do with Michael Caine?

He pushed Michael Caine to one side. What was he thinking about before? The gift. He had deceived Keziah, he had to admit. But now she was dead and would never know. Nonetheless, he now realised what he had done was wrong and that he had it within his power to put it right. He felt guilty as he thought about other things he had done or not done with her. There were so many things, but it was all too late: there wasn't anything he could do now about the past. But this one mistake he could redress in a few seconds.

Slowly and reluctantly, he logged into his account and checked his portfolio balance. He was worth, he realised with pleasure, nearly ten million pounds. His investments over the years had done very well, for he had started out as a vicar with much less than three million pounds saved from his previous job. Last year was the best run he had ever had. He could easily afford to make a really substantial gift. He went to send an email to the Woodland Trust and tell them – how pleased they would be – but as he did, he found that familiar hesitation again.

What was the point of throwing away his good money? The question lingered in his mind. He did want, he ruefully thought to himself, to make the gift, but when it came to doing it, he just couldn't. Nor could he reject the thought outright. He would, he resolved, have a further think and decide once and for all on Christmas Day.

Then yet again he thought of Michael Caine. Was he going mad? He liked him as an actor and a person and he enjoyed thinking of Caine's many films – Zulu, the Italian Job, Alfie, Get Carter – and then it suddenly came to him. Of course! Every year, he and Keziah loved watching Michael Caine as Scrooge in *The Muppet Christmas Carol*. Would that perhaps explain the strange frog?

Anyway, if he put it on quickly now, he could watch it before his Zoom call with his sisters, which he looked forward to more than anything. Rapidly he heated up a pizza and settled down to watch it. The experience was bittersweet. He had such happy memories of Keziah laughing uncontrollably at the Muppets fooling around, but he also battled with sadness and even bitterness at God or fate. They had removed that laughter so irretrievably. He felt terribly alone. But at the end of the film, he was also warmed by the familiar comforting story and felt strangely much better than he had before. Time to Zoom his sisters.

Chapter 8

Since he and Felix parted, Angus had been working hard. On Christmas Eve morning, he managed to arrange a meeting with his personal coach and then met his therapist in the afternoon. He could detoxify his body and his mind in one day if all went well.

George, his trainer, was based in a beautiful and historic set of buildings grouped around a quadrangle set into the Shoreham valley. They did some gentle stretching exercises, then ran along the river together and up the steep chalk downland slope beyond. The legality or otherwise of their activity in the latest government Covid announcement didn't seem to bother George in the least, who to Angus's surprise announced that he had no intention of being vaccinated.

'No way. The government is treating us like small children,' argued George as they ran uphill. 'Telling us to do this, don't do that. We need to stop being children and start behaving like adults. Everyone should take care of their own health, not have it dictated to them by these faceless bureaucrats.'

Angus puffed along behind. A big problem of discussing things with George was that he was never out of breath, no matter how fast he ran, whilst Angus was already panting like a dog.

'What about the people with . . . compromised immune systems? What are . . . they supposed to do?' he managed to reply.

'I feel for them, but they will have to stay inside until things calm down. Anyway, we are all going to have to die in the end,' proposed George.

'Doesn't that sound a bit like let them die . . . and reduce the surplus population?' Angus let out a harsh grunt.

George laughed. 'No, look, I'm very sympathetic to people who are genuinely ill, but most people of a certain age are responsible for their health. Obesity and smoking are the two biggest controllable factors in bad health. Too many people,' he looked at Angus with a small sympathetic smile, 'leave everything for years and then it's at risk of being too late.'

Angus now simply had to stop. He was breathing hard and leaned forward with his hands on his knees.

The view from the top was worth it: looking east, the whole valley below was set out like a picture book, while the hills rose like an image reflected in a mirror on the other side. They could see the village of Shoreham directly below, almost like an aerial photographic view laid out at their feet.

'So, you think everyone is overreacting?' Angus asked, still catching his breath.

George nodded. 'Oh yes, absolutely, and it's all being whipped up by fear. "Project Fear" is being rolled out yet again. Look, there is something to be concerned about: I'm not saying Covid isn't real, but 99.92% of people have nothing to be worried about. It's just like a severe cold, and we all must die in the end anyway. What I would do, if I was in charge, would be to say to people: "Look, here are the facts and this is the problem. You decide what to do." Some may carry on as normal, while others may decide to isolate. We should be encouraging people to take responsibility for their own health and take charge of their own life. Oversee your life, don't outsource it to the government.'

Angus thought for a moment. 'So, your view is like the poem I remember from school: "It matters not how strait the gate, How charged with punishments the scroll, I am the master of my fate: I am the captain of my soul."'

'Yes, exactly like that,' agreed George. 'Face death as a reality and try to put it off, if you can, by living in a healthy way. Accept the world as it is. Live as best you can in the meantime. Think about what you are doing with your body and the environment. Western science can prolong our life, but if we want to live fulfilled and enlightened lives then we need to look at the East and learn from the gurus about staring death in the face.'

Angus pondered over George's advice as they ran back. He wondered what Felix would have said in response. They ran much faster downhill, recrossed the river, which was swollen by rain, and then ran by the house where Samuel Palmer had painted his strange and dream-like visions of slumbering sheep and apple trees covered with blossoms. Finally, they ran back through the utterly deserted village

– which felt eerie, like the set for a remake of *The Midwich Cuckoos* – then up a steep path before turning sharply back on themselves and down a narrow lane to the gym. On their arrival, Angus nearly collapsed on his hands and knees.

As he got back in the car, he was still thinking about what George had said. It would be fascinating to see what his therapist said after lunch.

The therapist, Jonathan, was a short man with large glasses and a balding head. The light gleamed from his scalp and made his video a little distracting. They had only started working together recently. Angus had a somewhat chequered history with therapists – he started with them, then they fell out or he got bored. Like some football teams who loved to change their manager every few months, Angus was prone to chopping and changing.

Jonathan seemed to be a good therapist. He had started a few weeks ago by asking what brought Angus there and he felt Jonathan had really listened. At the last session, they talked about a word Angus had used in the previous session: 'I feel betrayed.'

Jonathan had asked him to explain what he meant. Angus wondered now in reply why this word was so fascinating.

'It's interesting that you've picked up on it again – were you thinking about that in the week? Did you have any further thoughts?' Jonathan asked.

'Well, it is a very strong word.' Angus responded, thinking. 'Betrayal is linked to treachery. It makes me think of Judas or Lord Haw-Haw.'

'Are you that angry with your ex-wives?'

Angus took a moment to digest the sudden deep dive before admitting, 'Maybe I am. Especially with the last one. I think she was, in retrospect, a bit of a gold digger. She certainly cleaned me out with the help of one of my biggest competitors, and that hurts both personally and professionally.'

'So, was it as much professional as personal?'

'Yes,' said Angus. 'I just hated the thought of Lewis and Threadmore and their juniors all sniggering. Not only about the amount they got out of me, but even more all the deeply personal details I had to disclose. Still, I suppose I'm getting a feeling for what it's like to be on the other side of the table.'

Jonathan paused, taking a minute to think. 'So, you are angrier with her lawyers than with Ros? How does it compare, the one anger to the other?'

Angus nodded. 'Definitely I'm angrier with them than her. I'm over her, and I never have to see her again as we have no children together, but I can't avoid running into that gruesome pair at cocktail parties. In fact, even before Covid, I'd stopped attending them. I can't stand people laughing at me.'

Jonathan looked at Angus. He asked, 'I'm curious, can you tell me more about why you feel like that?'

Angus grew impatient. 'Look, Jonathan, I've talked about this with previous counsellors, and I stopped with them because I felt we were endlessly going around in circles, always talking about feelings. You seem different, more, well, "business-like", and that appeals to me. I like to fix things and get things done, not talk endlessly about my feelings. So how do you think we can solve this, rather than all this fluffy discussion?'

Jonathan took another long breath. 'Well, maybe, I should take being called business-like as a backhanded compliment. Let's go further. What is it about being business-like that's appealing?'

There was silence.

Jonathan picked up again. 'I'm not here to fix you. That's not how counselling works. I will ask you this as a way to go further: please tell me what you imagine life would look like for you if counselling was successful. I know you are sceptical about counselling, and think it's all smoke and mirrors and letting your feelings hang out to dry, so let me explain what I'm trying to do. I wouldn't normally let a client "see my workings," but I will make an exception. What I'm trying to do is put the course of our counselling into your own hands, letting you be the person setting your own goals, giving you what we call in the counselling lingo "agency". Your life is your boat. You seem – to me, anyway – sceptical about everything, and in my experience people who are sceptics often have lost trust in themselves and they've given it away to someone else. It's always "someone else's fault". Rather, I want you to be able to trust the core of your being to find the truth, find something in this world and not give it up to others. What I mean is that it's *your* faith in something, not somebody else's. So, if you want to move on, what I'm asking you, again, is this: what would success look like?'

Angus nodded. 'Thank you, Jonathan, that's helpful. As a lawyer, I have a methodology I use with my clients, and it helps me to see yours. I can see that, unlike in law, counsellors are not trying to lead their clients. It's funny you use the word "faith", as I'm seeing an old friend tomorrow for Christmas who was a vicar and now has lost his faith, and here I am being told I need to find mine. I guess yes, I've become very cynical about life and women. I'd hoped that Ros was the one, but I had thought that about Sheena and Helen as well. Maybe I'm better off without women, or just having brief flings, but that doesn't seem to work either.' He paused, and neither spoke for a while, letting a silence sit between their laptops.

Angus continued. 'Your question is a really thought-provoking one, about what success would be like. I suppose it would look like this: a happy, loving, and loyal partner and a great relationship with my children. Currently, sadly, I have neither.'

Jonathan took a second before speaking. 'Thank you, Angus. I feel we are getting somewhere. Can you explain more, please, about what kind of relationship you would want with your children? What would be good?'

Angus didn't hesitate in his response. 'I feel so alienated from them, especially from Laura and Natalie. Not so much with Jack, but he has his own wholly separate life. He's got a successful technology start-up which absorbs his time. He's not angry with me like the other two are, he's just in his own cocoon . . . but then I guess I've been in mine, too, for a long time.'

Jonathan raised a hand. 'Let's take the easier one first, then. So, what would counselling change if it worked? What would be different about your relationship with Jack?'

'That we would spend more time with each other. That he would want to spend time with me. That we could talk honestly. But, in fairness, he's a chip off the old block. When he was small, I was never around either, and now he's grown up, I guess I'm getting a taste of my own medicine. My father was a bit the same as me, funnily enough: he was never around either. Are we all just trapped in an endless cycle?'

'No, we can change, and we are all responsible for our own actions. But it helps to understand why we do what we do. Look though, I'm sorry, but we shall have to leave it there. I'm afraid our time's up.'

They fixed a time for the second week of January and that was it. Angus was left staring at an empty screen. He poured himself a drink and caught up with his emails. Jonathan had made him think. He didn't want to continue like this. He must change – but how?

Chapter 9

Felix's sisters had been so helpful and kind to him since Keziah died. They had a WhatsApp group and every day without fail, over the last three years, they had messaged him. They asked him how he was doing, sent him funny memes to try and cheer him up, and had always been there for him, whatever his mood. Although all three were Christians, they had never once criticised him for his loss of faith, which he had felt able to tell them about – unlike with his parishioners, let alone his fellow clergy. They had been sympathetic and warm, trying to help but not judging him as he struggled with his doubts. He felt they were the only people he could be his real self around. He was incredibly grateful for their love and encouragement.

Although the three sisters were different in looks, on the phone they all sounded virtually the same, and they used to enjoy pulling Keziah's leg by pretending to be one of the others, sometimes for five minutes or more until they revealed their identity.

Having them all together on a Zoom call was a bit like standing in the centre of a warm and kind hurricane. They all spoke loudly and at the same time, and all constantly made funny comments or told amusing stories or contradicted what the previous sister had said. As they told these stories, they dissolved into laughter at their own jokes. Since childhood, they'd had nicknames for each other, some of which were quite rude and could be shocking to outsiders.

Most of all, they enjoyed arguing with each other and with Felix. This was the family's central pastime. It didn't matter what the subject was. In fact, they would cast around to find a suitable topic. After a typhoon of arguing vehemently backwards and forwards, suddenly without warning, peace would descend, and it would be as if no disagreement had ever taken place. Outsiders found it very hard to understand how one minute they could be at each other's throats and the next minute, there was an overflow of sibling love.

They had a custom for many years to tell each other a story of a Christmas gone past. It could be from their own childhood, stories told to them by their parents, or completely fictional. Every Christmas, their parents, and especially their father, had regaled them with tales of Christmas from his childhood during the Second World War in London.

After a few minutes of general catch-up on Zoom, they began. Felix went first.

'It's not a story per se, but what I can remember from Dad telling us about Christmas Day in around 1940. Christmas was always marked by the arrival of the maiden aunts on Christmas Eve: Grandma's sister and her mother's sister. Plus, of course, her mother herself. For these three ladies, this was the big event of the year. Otherwise, they rarely, if ever, went out. Oh, apart from the two-week summer seaside holiday with Dad's family – but of course, with the war, this hadn't happened that year. Though the aunts' arrival meant the children had to sleep on sofas and cushions, the three children loved having them. These elderly ladies dressed in an extraordinarily outdated Victorian fashion and were highly eccentric, and despite having little money, would generously slip sixpence into the children's hands when they thought their parents weren't looking. The children could be persuaded to tell embarrassing stories about their mother's childhood, but you had to time that when mother was asleep or in the kitchen or she would tell them to stop all that nonsense. Christmas morning, I recall that one year, Dad told us that David took a tray of tea first thing to his parents, plus a box of chocolates and a fulsome letter saying what wonderful parents they were. Dad and Margaret thought he was a complete creep!'

At that point, one of his sisters tried to interrupt, but Felix knew it would be a fatal mistake to give way – once you lost the pulpit, you could never get it back. He ploughed on.

'So, Grandfather and the children would go to church in the morning, but the ladies of the house would stay behind as they were cooking the Christmas lunch. Shocking. Even in the worst year of the war, such as 1941, there would be enough food to eat, as Mother would save up ration cards weeks ahead. After lunch, the family would always listen to the King's speech and then *A Christmas Carol* on the wireless. Margaret would be terrified of the ghosts as they appeared with suitably spectral sound effects. After that, they played charades and happy families. Then, finally, they would have a little "variety concert". One year, Margaret and Dad, who would have been perhaps eleven and eight, dressed up and sang, with accompaniment from David on the piano. They sang "Little Brown Jug", which is, if you know the lyrics, a lot of jokes about an alcoholic couple. Despite Grandfather's strict teetotalism – even sherry trifle was banned – it brought the house down and Grandfather himself was shaking uncontrollably with laughter. Then, on Boxing Day, Uncle Horace and his wife Emily would come for lunch. The children loved him but disliked her, as he was as generous as she was mean. On one occasion Horace gave one of them half a crown, and she made him take it back. The Christmas puddings, as you know, contained silver three penny bits wrapped in greaseproof paper, which could be redeemed for a penny. Horace, who was a joker, pretended one year to have found a ten-shilling note in the pudding. There were three enormous homemade Christmas puddings: one for Christmas Day, one for Boxing Day, and one for Grandpa's birthday which was April 4th.'

As soon as he finished, Felix's story unleashed a barrage of corrections, amendments, contradictions and clarifications.

Next came Esther. She was the eldest and lived in the North.

'Since we were talking about a Christmas pudding lottery, here is the famous story of the Christmas turkey raffle. Opposite Dad's home lived the Albrightons. Grandpa approved of them as Mr Albrighton was a Captain in the regular army, admittedly in the Catering Corps, not the Grenadier Guards – but still, as Grandpa pointed out, the army needed feeding. In 1943, which was the hardest winter of the war, Grandma had her work cut out to find meat for Christmas lunch. Vegetables were fine from Grandpa's allotment, but all meat was hard to find and very expensive, which was important as the meat was rationed by price. Even meat that was available, like sausages, was of dubious quality – it was more bread than meat. Then, a week before Christmas, there was a light knock on the kitchen door, and there was Mrs Albrighton clutching a large bag.

"My husband has just got an extra turkey and we have two already. Would you like it?" Grandma hesitated and Mrs Albrighton, who was a kind soul, stepped inside.

"Don't worry, it didn't fall off the back of a lorry. They had some extra food at work, so they had a raffle and Charles got a turkey. Please take it. We've two already, and you've got all those extra mouths to feed." Grandma gratefully accepted, to the delight of the children, but when Grandpa came home from work, there was a problem. A big problem. He was immediately suspicious about the provenance of the magnificent bird and cross-questioned Grandma about how she got it. The fatal word "raffle" crossed her lips and could not be unsaid.

"I'm sorry," said Grandpa firmly, "we shall have to return it. It's out of the question to eat turkey won in a raffle." The children were so upset but Grandpa's will was like the law of the Medes and Persians. Once made, it could not be changed.

Grandma, though, was a smart and resourceful character, so the next morning she packed up the turkey and crossed the road. The children watching her through the window were sad. The pitifully small chicken they had would hardly feed eight of them. A few minutes passed and Grandma returned. Again, carrying a turkey. Grandma just smiled enigmatically when they asked what had happened. "Just wait," she said.

On Grandpa's return from work early on Christmas Eve, before the elderly ladies arrived, he, to the children's surprise, nervously asked, "Did you sort out the turkey?"

"Oh yes," replied Grandma. "Come and see."

The whole family trooped into the kitchen and there on the side was a splendid turkey ready to be cooked.

"But I thought we had agreed that we couldn't have a turkey we'd won on a raffle."

Grandma paused and smiled. "This turkey was NOT won in a raffle."

She looked around triumphantly. "This is not a raffle turkey, this is a gift turkey. I explained our predicament to kind Mrs Albrighton, who promptly and simultaneously took back the turkey she'd won in a raffle and gave me as a free gift her second spare turkey. This turkey can be eaten."

There was silence in the kitchen. The children looked anxiously at their father. He stepped forward and hugged his wife. As the children later tucked into the splendid bird, they gazed lovingly and admiringly at their resourceful mother.'

They all knew this story back to front and in various versions. The ending in particular was subject to change, but it was agreed after some arguments that this was both the truest and the best variant.

Next came Hannah. She was the middle sister and a teacher.

'My story is not about turkey but Turkey. It was the winter of 62 or 63, so only Felix was alive, and Esther was en route. On Christmas Eve 1962, Dad got a phone call from a friend of his, who was a missionary in Turkey. A Turkish man was alone in London. Could he come down and spend Christmas with them? Of course, the answer was yes, and Dad met him at the station on the last train of Christmas Eve. Though there was no snow, it was already bitterly cold, and Dad's ancient Wolseley slithered on the ice down the lanes to their house. They put him to sleep in the box room, but as you know the house had a very sloping roof and being tucked under the eaves didn't suit our claustrophobic visitor at all. In the middle of the night, he woke our parents up. They swapped Felix with him, and Felix had the nicest room of all of us and never had to share. So, the Turkish guest slept well. Christmas Day the next morning was even colder, but again no snow. They walked over the fields to church, the frozen ground crunching under their feet. Despite never having been in a church, the guest enjoyed the service and absolutely loved Christmas lunch. The only awkward point came in the afternoon when they played with their neighbours, the James', the good old board game "Diplomacy". To everyone's embarrassment, the Turkish guest was annoyed at the depiction of the Turkish Sultan as an obese figure smoking a hookah pipe. After some unsuccessful efforts to soothe his aggrieved feelings, it was agreed they would play Monopoly instead. It would be a relief when this slightly awkward but not unfriendly guest would be leaving early on Boxing Day morning . . . but it was not to be, as the day dawned to heavy snow. The lane leading to the main road was utterly impassable, and was to remain so until early March. Things became, as you all know, so snowbound that milk and other supplies had to be fetched by sledge from the village a few miles away. Suddenly, the Turkish man revealed an unexpected side to his character. This kind of snow was very normal, he explained, in his home city in Eastern Turkey. He loved the snow and was more than willing – in fact, he would be delighted – to pull the sledge over the fields for supplies. This is what he did for two months, earning our parents' deep gratitude, especially as Mum was heavily pregnant, until eventually, the snow began to melt, and he could return to London. During that period, they learned of his past, his family and how he came to be in England. But that is another story.'

Finally, it was Rachel's turn. She was the baby of the family and a nurse.

'My story is a short one, and one we can all remember. Christmas morning, and it must have been 1977 or 1978. Dad complained over breakfast that he didn't feel well, and by mid-morning he was in real pain, writhing around in agony on the floor surrounded by half-opened presents, which we callous children were anxious to open. Dad had refused to call the GP as it was Christmas Day, and he didn't want to bother him or disrupt our Christmas. Eventually, he gave way and allowed Mum to call. Within 30 minutes, the GP was there. Imagine today, he'd have to have waited on a plastic A&E chair for four hours. Anyway, the doctor immediately diagnosed kidney stones.

"Here are some painkillers. Drink as much water as you can and go to bed."

Dad did, and by late afternoon he was feeling better and able to lie on the green sofa under a blanket while we finished opening our presents. Looking back, what strikes me is the love that our parents had for us. They had many troubles of their own we didn't know about, but that sadness was subsumed by their love for us and others, like in the last story. Now I have children of my own, I realise this deep parental love isn't automatic, and how fortunate we were as children to have experienced it. You read these terrible stories of children tortured and starved to death by their own parents and realise how blessed we are. That's why I love Christmas so much, and love Christmas stories of kindness and generosity and love.' She paused. 'I recently read a short story by Tolstoy called "Where Love is, God is." That sums up what I've been trying to say. Do read it, dearest Felix, and it will do you good.'

After this, they chatted further, and when they eventually signed off, Felix felt his soul warmed and comforted. He went to bed content.

Chapter 10

Felix slept well, lulled by the heartwarming stories from the previous night, and got up very early on Christmas morning.

He couldn't face going to the early Christmas service, but he would, he decided, go to see the church. It was still dark as he crossed the graveyard that separated the vicarage from the church. Nobody was around, he was relieved to see, and although the church was locked, he still had the keys. He stepped into the pulpit and looked around at the empty expectant pews.

Here, he had told his congregation for so many years the Christmas story, as his predecessors had done for countless generations before. There was even a list of them going back to 1454. He recalled that the oldest part of the building was supposedly Saxon. Outside was a holy well dedicated to the Saxon princess St Edith, the illegitimate daughter of King Edgar. But there were Roman settlements nearby which had been excavated with Christian mosaics, so it was quite possible that Christmas had been celebrated here or nearby for getting on two thousand years – in fact, only a few centuries after the birth itself.

And here he was, still the vicar of Kemsing, charged with passing the news on as part of an unbroken chain, yet now utterly unable to say anything. Last Christmas, although his doubts were growing, he had taken the service as normal and been amazed by his ability to preach something he only half believed. He had winced internally when many of the congregation had bustled up to him afterwards to say how much they enjoyed his talk.

There was, he realised later, a deep well of affection towards him and a feeling of, he guessed, solidarity that he had to preach on such a sad anniversary. He thought particularly of his two churchwardens. They were both very busy people, yet they had so lovingly made time to try and help him and were always dropping by to give him food or see how he was doing. The love and care of the people from his church for him was something, he realised, that meant a lot.

The thing that struck him as he stood in the pulpit was the absolute silence. The church was silent, but more than that, God himself seemed to be silent. The congregation would speak later but from the divine source of it all, nothing seemed to come.

Felix recalled a book he had read and enjoyed as a student: *He is There and He is Not Silent*.

Grimly, he thought to himself, the title needed changing to something like *Is He There and Why is He Silent?*

As he was leaving the church, two ladies of the church were coming the other way up the path, carrying huge armfuls of Christmas wreaths and fresh ivy and fir boughs. So large was the greenery that they looked like walking bushes.

He just about recognised them – Jo and Vanessa.

'Good morning, Felix, and a Merry Christmas to you,' they cheerily said to him, and were obviously just about to ask him how he was doing, so he mumbled an excuse and almost fled back to the vicarage through the graveyard in case he met anyone else.

He reproached himself as he opened the wicket gate at the side of the graveyard that led to the vicarage. He was stupid. Why was he so afraid of talking about himself, let alone about Keziah? Reproachfully he thought that Jo and Vanessa, who were so kind and had also supported him so loyally, might have been about to say something kind and helpful.

This day of all days was especially painful for him, like a raw untreated wound, and would forever be ruined for him by the memories of her death. Every Christmas was like a stab in the heart. How cruel of God to allow that. If there was a loving God, how could he do that? If he had wanted to take her, why that day? And if he had done it then, why didn't he do something now to make it better? And if he couldn't or wouldn't do something, then why wouldn't he at least say something?

Safely back indoors, he felt hungry, and thought it was time for breakfast. Could he face some Christmas music? He had a Christmas playlist that he and Keziah had built up over the years, but it might be too much for him to play and it wouldn't be good to be tear stained when Angus appeared. Angus's generous offer struck him. How strange that the atheist should be the helper, that the one person who wouldn't leave him alone was not a Christian but decidedly and dogmatically anti-Christian.

He decided he would just play one carol, her favourite, the one he'd thought about yesterday. It was a rather obscure hymn, rarely sung now, called 'Christians Awake'. He smiled to himself when he remembered how one year, she had muddled up the title and asked him to play 'Christians, Wake Up'.

The music played, but he wasn't really listening to the words, until despite himself the same verse caught his attention.

'Oh, may we keep and ponder in our mind
God's wondrous love in saving lost mankind!
Trace we the babe, who hath retrieved our loss,
from his poor manger to his bitter cross.
Tread in his steps, assisted by his grace,
till our imperfect state God doth replace.

Yes, he thought. That was what he needed: his loss retrieved – things reversed that should never have happened. Christmas Day three years ago, Keziah was in bed, struggling to breathe, her pale drawn face etched with grey, the hospice staff carefully and gently moving around, knowing it was nearly the end.

'So, baby Jesus,' thought Felix, 'yes, go ahead, please retrieve my loss. Make right what's gone wrong. Help me.'

He made himself some breakfast, and as he did, he thought of the Tolstoy story that his sister had recommended last night. He quickly found it on Google and was amused to find, first of all, that Tolstoy had gotten into trouble for plagiarism, having brazenly lifted the original story from a French pastor without any attempt to credit him.

The story tells of a humble Russian cobbler, Martin, who is struggling after the death of his son. He is told miraculously that Christ will visit him, but instead of Christ coming he receives a stream of needy visitors. The cobbler is looking for Christ, but in the meantime, he takes care of this string of poor people. Then, only at the end, is it revealed to him that the poor were Christ in disguise and that in welcoming them, he was welcoming Christ.

But it was the start of the story that particularly struck him. He reread it. Martin complained to a holy man:

'"All I ask of God is that I soon may die. I am now quite without hope in the world."

The old man replied: "You have no right to say such things, Martin. We cannot judge God's ways. Not our reasoning, but God's will, decides. As to your despair, that comes because you wish to live for your own happiness."

"What else should one live for?" asked Martin.

"For God, Martin," said the old man. "He gives you life, and you must live for Him. When you have learnt to live for Him, you will grieve no more, and all will seem easy to you."

Martin was silent awhile, and then asked: "But how is one to live for God?"

The old man answered: "How one may live for God has been shown us by Christ. Can you read? Then buy the Gospels and read them."'

'Well,' said Felix to himself, 'that's a curious story, because I am quite like Martin in a way. What I certainly would like is some hope. That's what I'm missing now: hope.

"We cannot judge God's ways." For me now, I don't want to judge his ways, but I do want to understand his ways or have them explained to me, at least in part. Can't God give me that? But on the other hand, I've never heard any miraculous voices and anyway, it's just a story, the same way *A Christmas Carol* is just a story. And maybe the same way the gospels is just a story. I don't need fairy stories, I need reality. And besides which,' he continued to mumble to himself, a wave of cynicism washing over him, 'both Tolstoy and Dickens preached this wonderful, attractive idea of brotherly love, which is admirable, but both treated their wives abominably. They couldn't live up to what they preached. What miserable hypocrites they were, and I guess what a miserable hypocrite I have been – telling people things I don't believe myself.'

He made up a picnic with traditional Christmas food: turkey sandwiches, pigs in blankets; mince pies, and even a few Brussels sprouts. To drink, he found a bottle of red wine that he'd been saving for a picnic with Keziah which never happened. Angus would no doubt have enough alcoholic beverages for ten of them. He dusted off an old picnic blanket to sit on. The weather was sunny but cold. He didn't mind the chill but would wrap up in multiple layers, as Keziah often instructed.

Just then the doorbell rang, and it was Angus. He was standing there, smiling broadly and armed with a giant rucksack which, judging by the shapes bulging from the side of it, contained enough food and especially enough drink for a serious polar expedition.

Chapter 11

Felix and Angus left the vicarage.

Felix was afraid of running into more people like Jo and Vanessa, so after looking both ways, they took the least frequented path and went again due east, passing behind the church and entering the recreation ground. The huge space was completely empty apart from a few dog walkers in the far distance. They aimed for the far northeast corner of the Rec, where they then came out on an exceptionally narrow road. Barely big enough for one vehicle, there was almost nowhere to pass, and Felix had a few times seen queues of traffic piled up behind white vans; the drivers often argued with each other about who should reverse.

But now the lane was empty and quiet. The sound of their walking boots on the tarmac echoed from the high hedges on either side. They then came to a crossroad marked by a yellow salt box and turned left. The road was lined by hedges at the top of steep banks and was a heavy incline. After some minutes of toiling upward, they were both breathless.

To the west, they could see a far country through occasional gaps in the banks and hedges. The views were exceptional, as the rising sun lit up the hills to the south in its rays. The delectable vista was only slightly marred by the M26 in the valley below, but even that housed very few cars. As they climbed further after a while, they could see that the lane began to wind steeply into the oncoming trees. There was a broad gate just before the road turned and leaning on his staff, looking at the sheep in the pasture was an old man, whom Felix recognised as Brian.

Brian had lived with his wife in his cottage off to the right for many years and wrote the highly popular nature comments in the Kemsing parish magazine.

'Merry Christmas, vicar,' Brian said with a cheery wave.

'And to you, dear Brian,' Felix replied, introducing Angus. 'Anything interesting to see?'

'Birds of prey mainly, Felix,' observed Brian, pointing. 'See those buzzards circling over the wood over there? They're looking for their Christmas dinner of mice!'

The three men looked at the view; the sun rising increased the golden colouring of the hills in the far distance. With a stab of pain and recognition, Felix realised he could just about make out the hills which formed the summit of Emmetts, a National Trust property, which he and Keziah had loved to visit. Many times, they had stood there, and she had said, 'Look, darling, you can see for miles – even as far as the Green Hill of Kemsing.'

Such happy memories of walking hand in hand with her through the verdant meadow flowers at Emmetts. Of having tea and a sausage roll. Of laughing at his lamentable botanical knowledge.

As he recalled these and many more, a wave of deep feelings surged over him. A sense of longing and grief mixed, almost to his surprise, with something like laughter; the feeling of a mighty wave engulfing a small boy on a beach. He staggered and almost fell. Angus reached out a kindly hand and steadied him.

'I'm ok, thanks,' said Felix in response to the unspoken question from his friend. Brian looked at him sympathetically.

'Fair knocks you out that view,' he said.

'Sorry both, it's just memories of days gone past,' Felix mumbled.

'Don't worry. We've missed you, vicar,' said Brian slowly and deliberately. 'Be lovely if you could stay here a bit longer. Don't go unless you feel you must. I'm sure you know how much folk appreciate you.'

Felix didn't know what to say to the kind old shepherd.

'Thank you, Brian,' he said, feeling the need to move on. 'You are such an encouragement. Have a wonderful Christmas yourself.'

Brian waited until they were moving up the road again before exclaiming, 'Godspeed to you both.'

'What a charming man,' said Angus as they walked away.

'He and his wife have been such an encouragement to me ever since I got here. Churches, especially rural churches, can be so tricky. Someone once asked me, "Did I ever think about resigning?" and I said, "Only once a month for twenty years." Everyone views it as their church, and God forbid you try and change anything. But what you need then is a few Brian's – or Jo and Vanessa's – to keep you going.'

Now as the two went on, the road became again very narrow, twisting backwards and forwards. The sun disappeared behind the trees and it quickly became cold, bitterly cold. On the right, the ground plunged down to the east, while on the left, the thickly wooded half frozen slopes rose from the top of the green bank. The autumnal trees grew tighter and tighter overhead until they were walking in a yellow tunnel; enough leaves had lasted from autumn to give shelter.

As they rounded a bend, they saw that on a large tree on the right, which stretched out over the road, were hundreds of pairs of shoes, laces tied together, hanging from the branches. Felix had seen the tree before, though every time he came by there were more pairs of shoes. This was all new to Angus and he was entranced.

'Who on earth did that and what does it mean?'

'There are multiple theories,' Felix responded, 'and it's even been debated in the letters page of the Sevenoaks Chronicle. Some people say it's a sign of fertility, while some argue the opposite, that it's a sign of someone's death. Another theory is that this is a place to deal drugs, which I have to say is laughable, as I can hardly think of a less likely place. My theory is that what started as a few local youths playing a prank has grown in the telling and acquired a life of its own. Nobody really knows, and I don't suppose we ever will.'

'A prank that acquired a life of its own? Maybe like the gospels then?' Angus grinned.

Felix felt he had to defend what he wasn't sure he believed, but he couldn't let Angus win.

'I can give you a very well-researched book on that, Angus, written by my good friend, Professor Peter Williams, if you like.'

'No, thank you. I'm fine for kindling at the moment.'

They both laughed and continued up the hill. On the left, just short of the brow, was a narrow lane marked 'North Downs Way'. This was the way they took. The track was cobbled and indented with little rivulets caused by rain finding its own route down the hill. After a few hundred yards, the track turned up to the right and they climbed over a stile into a field.

As they climbed down, almost out of nowhere, a hiker with a huge pack on his back appeared alongside them. Felix wondered whether he'd been walking on the parallel path and wanted to wish them a Merry Christmas.

Chapter 12

Without any invitation from Felix and Angus, the hiker immediately started walking side by side with them. Felix, who was now in the middle of the three men, found this odd. They hadn't invited him; he'd unexpectedly shown up and just inserted himself into their group. He shot a glance at the hiker to see what he was up to, but his face was half hidden under a hoodie. What he could see revealed a younger man, bearded, with a dark face. He didn't look English and in fact, he couldn't be, or he wouldn't have attached himself to them uninvited.

'I could hear you talking as you joined the path,' said the hiker and now Felix could tell from his accent that he certainly wasn't English. He'd hazard a guess that he was Middle Eastern. Kurdish or Syrian? Maybe he was a refugee who'd landed in Kent on a boat, Felix pondered, remembering the waves of arrivals that had been all over the BBC news a couple of nights ago. So perhaps he was a refugee heading for London, but if so, this was a very strange route to take.

'What were you discussing as you walked along together?'

This was even more ignorant of English social customs and Felix was slightly annoyed. He and Angus stopped. It was none of his business. Maybe they should shake off this intrusive visitor. Felix didn't want to confront the stranger directly, but he did want to indicate his discomfiture with his intrusion, so he deliberately looked away from him, staring intently down at the ground, focusing on a clump of grass.

'Oh, all the things that have been going on these days.'

'What things?' the hiker asked.

Felix couldn't help but laugh. 'What things? Have you just landed here from Mars? You must know: all the sadness and misery in the world, which has been made ten times worse by this stupid Covid, which means we can't have Christmas lunch with our loved ones as we do in this country every year, instead reduced to hiking to nowhere with a few sausage rolls for a lonely lunch.'

The hiker seemed seemingly puzzled. 'But I thought it was your Christmas festival today? Shouldn't you be happy and joyful?'

At this, they both jumped in.

Angus snorted and said, slightly ahead of Felix, 'Ha! I don't believe in Christmas anyway.'

Felix said over Angus, 'Well, I was a believer in Christmas in days gone by, but now I'm just sad, to be honest. My friend doesn't believe it and I don't know whether I believe it or not.'

'What's changed your mind?' asked the hiker, looking at Felix, 'What don't you believe in?' he asked again, turning to Angus.

'I was a vicar,' Felix decided to respond. 'Well, I guess technically I still am – so for many years I've told my people at Christmas about the baby in the manger being the Son of God. "Peace on earth and goodwill to men." You must know the sort of thing. But then something evil happened to me – my wife died three years ago today of cancer – and it's knocked me for six. I asked God for help, but none came. If he had cared, surely he would have shown up and done something. Having said that, if you'd asked me a week ago, I would have told you it was all a complete fairy story. Now I'm not so sure what I think. Some strange things have happened to me in the last few days, which made me think again. Besides that, I have three sisters and I was talking to them last night. It is curious how they have this amazingly vibrant faith and love of Christmas, which I find very attractive. One of them recommended Tolstoy's story "Where Love is, God is" and I just read it and it struck me. I'd like to have faith too, as I once did, but I can't find it again. I'm stuck.'

'How about you?' the hiker asked Angus.

'Oh, none of it makes any sense to me at all.' Angus smiled. 'Never has. I'm not a religious person and often like to poke fun at it. The church is packed from top to bottom with hypocrites. But I do feel sorry for my friend here, Felix. I'm Angus, by the way. His faith was so helpful to him, even though I didn't think it was true. Now I can't even pull his leg about it. But how about you? What's your name? Are you a Christian, or even perhaps a priest? And, if you don't mind me asking you so directly: who are you and what are you doing here high on the Downs and where are you from and where are you going? Are you a tourist? A long-distance hiker? A refugee? A pilgrim?'

The hiker chuckled. 'I'm a bit of all of those, and I've certainly been a refugee. I've got some work to carry out this Christmas morning, which is why I'm here. I'm not a follower of Christ, if that's what being a Christian means, but I am rather familiar with the Bible. See, I think that's where your problem lies – for both of you in fact. You are so cold-hearted and slow – especially Felix, as you know it so well – to believe what the Bible says about Jesus and Christmas.'

At that, Felix couldn't help but jump in.

'But there's hardly anything about Christmas in the Bible, anyway. Just a few verses in a couple of books about shepherds and wise men and angels.'

'Are you sure?' the hiker replied. 'There's much more than you might think. Consider, for example, the first chapter of John. It doesn't mention Christmas or baby Jesus or a manger, but in fact, it's all about Jesus's arrival and why he came. Take this verse, for example:

"The word became flesh and made his dwelling among us, and we have seen his glory, the glory of the one and only son who came from the father full of grace and truth." That's Christmas in a nutshell.'

With that, he started to explain to them in detail the first part of John I. Felix had heard this passage many times, and even Angus was vaguely familiar with it, but they had never heard it taught or explained like this before. The hiker invited as many questions as they wanted and didn't seem to mind their constant interruptions. He also often laughed at their questions, sometimes almost shaking with mirth. On other occasions, though, he rebuked Felix, sharply.

'Really, Felix, as a vicar you should know that. You are a teacher of the English, so you of all people should know it.'

They had never had a conversation remotely like it. They were transfixed. The hiker finished his explanation by saying, 'So if you want to find, or rediscover and experience God, know him, taste him and see him, talk to him as closely as we are talking now, then how to do that is simply to read one of the gospels. As I believe Tolstoy's holy man recommended, Felix. Faith isn't a leap in the dark, it's looking at evidence and figuring out if it's true or not.'

Chapter 13

'Thank you so much for explaining that. It was fascinating,' said Angus. 'But can I ask another question? I'm sorry, I still don't get Christmas. I don't mean the commercial razzmatazz: that's just annoying. What I mean is I still don't get the Christmas story itself. What you said was very thought-provoking, but when I hear it from Felix and his crew, it's not the same at all. It's nice and sweet and all that "away in a manger" and so on. It's lovely for small children, but they grow up and become adults like me and what does it possibly have to do with me today in 2020?'

The hiker paused again and looked at Angus steadily. 'Sweet? What, sweet like Herod killing all the boy babies? Sweet like two terrified parents being forced to flee him and become refugees in a strange land? Imagine what it was like to escape a murderous tyrant and arrive penniless in a foreign country where nobody speaks your language and where nobody really cares. And Jesus continues like that his whole life – "for the Son of Man has nowhere to lay his head".

'You've made it sentimental and cosy – I really do blame things like "Away in a Manger" and *A Christmas Carol* for that – but for the people there two thousand years ago, it was shot through with suffering. Where is the suffering in your Christmas?'

Angus wasn't convinced. 'Ok, I admit we've made it sugary sweet, but if it's not about saying "awh" to baby Jesus then, what is it about? Despite my best efforts not to, I funnily enough feel very sorry for the refugees today, and I have to say I'm glad we've met you. Even though I'm not religious, I find it fascinating to listen to you.' He paused. 'Maybe in a bit you'd like to share our food when we stop for a picnic? I've more than enough for you as well, and I'd really like it if you could.'

Felix nodded his head.

'But here's the thing,' continued Angus, 'yes, I can see we have not seen the true meaning of Christmas, it's been lost in all the tinsel. I now understand more about what John's gospel means. But that brings me to this: so, what? What's the message for me? What's it got to say to me Angus, now, today on the 25th December 2020?'

The hiker paused and looked carefully at them both, smiling.

'Listen carefully. There was a man called Athanasius, writing not long after Jesus was on Earth, and he said this: "Christ became what we are, that we might become what he is."

'If you think about it, this is what it's all about: an amazing exchange. Jesus – "God with us" – enters your life so you might enter his. God the Son becomes your brother, so you may become a son or daughter of the living God. That brother, Jesus, has come to make us part of the family of God. How does our brother do it? He becomes "one" with his siblings, taking all that is theirs. He arrives just as they do and takes on everything they have, except the evil inside every human being. And he does this to accomplish his mission: to finally take upon himself at the cross the one remaining thing, even that dreaded enemy of evil, sin and death. The one thing you can't solve, he will deal with. He will stop at nothing to be with you and rescue you. And he will suffer for this act, suffer far beyond anything you can imagine.

'So, this is the great exchange: God became human and was and is as we are, including even taking the consequences of our sin, so that we can become as he is and come home to the Father.'

Felix jumped in. 'I like that very much, thank you for making it sound so straightforward I guess, and that all sounds great in general. But I have the same question as Angus: what do you say to me in particular? Where was that great exchange – in fact, where was Jesus – when I was beside my wife dying of cancer on this day, on Christmas Day, three years ago? On that day of all days. Why is God persecuting me and killing me so relentlessly? Why does he shut his door? At least talk to me, even if it's to tell me to go away. I ask him, I cry to him, but I get back . . . nothing.' Felix almost spat out the last word.

The hiker put his hand on Felix's shoulder. The touch felt warm, even through the many layers.

'I'm so sorry, my brother. This life is a vale of tears. You are, I can see, walking through the valley of the shadow of death. If you need his presence, have you considered that even though you can't feel him, he may nonetheless be there? He's not far from each one of us but our senses might not alert us to him.' He paused. 'But don't misunderstand me, Felix – I'm also genuinely and deeply moved by your loss.'

Felix looked at him, struck by the deep sincerity in his voice, and noticed with surprise that the man's eyes were glistening with tears as he spoke.

Felix felt something shift in him. 'Thank you. That means a lot, that someone who doesn't know me from Adam is so kind. But please sir, help me with this.'

It did strike Felix as strange that a vicar with multiple theological qualifications was being instructed by someone who appeared to be a young Kurdish or whatever refugee with presumably no degrees whatsoever.

'Why all this suffering in the first place? Why couldn't God just make it right without all this hoo-hah?' Felix winced, and realised he had made a mistake, for the hiker looked at him strangely. 'I'm sorry that's the wrong word, my apologies. Let me have a second chance to put that more clearly – why did Christ need to suffer?'

The hiker stopped walking and looked at them with a burning intensity. 'That is so important. Here's something to help you:

'"But we do see Jesus, who was made lower than the angels for a little while, now crowned with glory and honour because he suffered death so that by the grace of God he might taste death for everyone. In bringing many sons and daughters to glory, it was fitting that God, for whom and through whom everything exists, should make the pioneer of their salvation perfect through what he suffered. Both the one who makes people holy and those who are made holy are of the same family. So, Jesus is not ashamed to call them brothers and sisters."

'God chose the way of tasting death as it is the only way. You see, it was fitting, or we might say as, I think, Jesus himself said somewhere,' the hiker laughed, 'that it was necessary for Christ to suffer. A man called Dietrich Bonhoeffer was about to be executed in 1945 and out of his jail cell he smuggled a little piece of paper and on it, he wrote these words: "Only a suffering God can help us." That's the nub of it: the baby in the manger came to be with us, suffer with us, die with us, came to raise us to life. But Christmas is not only about suffering, even more it is about healing.

'"Jesus bore our sins in his body on the tree, so that we might die to evil and live to what is right. By his wounds, you have been healed."

'He suffered as a human being and that means he knows what suffering is like and can help you with it.'

They walked on a bit further in silence. Then the stranger stopped and looked at them, and his eyes sparkled.

'So, friends, feel free to ask me what you like, but I suggest now, as it's Christmas, let's look down together into the manger. What do we see? We see this. He who was rich beyond all counting for our sakes became very poor. Being in very nature God, he made himself nothing. The Word became flesh.'

He knelt on the ground and looked up at them with a smile. 'See how low he comes: not to your level – and that would be amazing enough – but below you, so you are looking down at him. Behold the glory of the "little" Lord Jesus. So, what should Christmas be? Christmas should be this. The time we point down to a manger and say: "Look! God has shown up to put things right." In becoming man, the Lord of all has taken the wheel of this world, switched on the GPS, and pressed: "Home." You said you were like a car crashed into a ditch; Christ is the car mechanic coming to tow us out and put us on the road to home. You shy away from the lowliness and suffering of Christmas, and Covid and cancer, because you prefer a story of glory. A story of glory is about a ladder to heaven, ascending to God through our strength. But Christmas is the exact opposite: it's a story of a baby coming down, the manger and the cross, about God's descent to us in our utter helplessness, to pull us out of the ditch.'

Angus jumped in. 'I have another question, then, if you don't mind. Why does God hide? Why doesn't he make it more obvious? I'm a lawyer, and I look for facts. If the facts are staring you in the face, then I recognise them and I change my mind.'

'Now, is that so?' The hiker looked fixedly at Angus, so much so that Angus couldn't help but blush.

'Let me tell you a story.

'There once was a king who loved a humble maiden. She had no royal pedigree, no education, and no standing in the royal court. She dressed in rags. She lived in a hovel; she lived the ragged life of a peasant. But for reasons no one could quite figure out, the king fell in love with this girl. Why he should love her was beyond explaining, but love her he did, and he could not stop loving her. She was to become his queen, and it would be done. For he was a man of immense power.

This poor peasant girl would have no power to resist; she would have to become the queen.

'But there awoke in the heart of the king an anxious thought: "How in the world am I going to reveal my love to this girl? How can I bridge the chasm that separates us?" His advisers, of course, told him that all he had to do was command.

'But power, even unlimited power, cannot command love. The king could force her body to be present in the palace, but he could not force love to be present in her heart. He longed for the intimacy of heart and oneness of spirit, and all the power in the world cannot unlock the human heart—it must be opened from within.

'So, he met with his advisers once again, and they suggested he try to bridge the chasm by elevating her to his position. He could shower her with gifts, dress her in purple and silk, and have her crowned the queen. But if he brought her to his palace, if she saw all the wealth, pomp, and power of his greatness, then she would be overwhelmed. How would he ever know if she loved him for himself, or for all that he had given her? And how could she know that he loved her and would love her still if she had remained only a humble peasant?

'There was only one way. So one day, the king arose, took off his crown, relinquished his sceptre, laid aside his royal robes, and took upon himself the life of a peasant. He dressed in rags, scratched out a living in the dirt, grovelled for food, and dwelt in a hovel.

'He did not just take on the outward appearance of a servant, he became a servant – it was his actual life, his actual nature, his actual burden. He became as ragged as the one he loved so that she could be his forever. It was the only way. His ruggedness became the very signature of his presence.

'And so it is when God seeks to gain the freely-given love of human beings.'

Angus didn't know what to say, so they simply walked on together in silence. They came to the end of the fields and climbed over a narrow stile. Now the path ran straight between two wooded areas. On the right, the trees ran as far as the eye could see. Though the leaves had fallen, there remained a carpet of yellow and orange. On the left, though, they were much narrower and through the bare trees; you could see a wooded pasture sloping down steeply to the valley. In the middle of the pasture ran a line of majestic beech trees, like sentinels guarding the path against any dangers.

Felix turned to the hiker, surprising himself with his words. 'Can I ask you another question? I've got something on my mind that I feel bad about. My late wife asked me to donate to the Woodland Trust for tree planting, which I did, but I deliberately deceived her about how much we had to give and gave far less than I should have. What should I do? It's been preying on my mind all week.'

The hiker considered this and was silent for a minute, looking at the ground. 'Well, you can't ask her to forgive you, but you can ask God. What we do wrong is most of all against him. And you can still put right what's wrong – how much do you think you should give to do that?'

Felix was very unwilling to let Angus know how much money he had, so he simply said, 'Well, maybe five or ten times what I gave originally.'

'Whatever you feel is right, do it, and when you've done it, go and enjoy the newly planted trees and you will see that they will clap their hands in joy.'

Felix felt a relief drop from his shoulders, as if a burden he'd been carrying was rolled away.

Angus was listening carefully. 'Well, what about me?' he said. 'My problem is a lot more complicated than my tree-hugging friend here. I'm estranged in one way or another from my three children. It's my own fault, I guess, to some extent: I neglected them when they were young and spent all my time on work. Now I want to repair things.'

The hiker looked at Angus. 'As with your friend, your greatest need is to get right with God. And yes, I know you don't believe in him. But though you may not be looking for him, he is looking for you. You have an advantage over Felix in that you can do what he can't do. Ask for forgiveness. Go to your children and say, "I've sinned against heaven and against you and I'm sorry, how can we make it better?" Once we can do that, you will be amazed at what can happen next.'

Both men pondered over the advice and independently thought how odd it was they were unburdening their souls to a random Middle Eastern refugee. But, of course, they didn't say that out loud.

After a short while, as they walked on together, they found a tumbledown, open-sided shelter, nestling against the opening to a much larger wood.

'I know the man who owns this wood and pasture – he lives back that way,' Felix explained, pointing. 'He sadly doesn't come to Kemsing church; he drives past us to Sevenoaks, but never mind. I'm sure he wouldn't mind us using it. Look, there are even some logs we can sit on and one we can use as a sort of table. Please, friend, join us.'

Angus agreed, and the two urged him to stay with them. However, the hiker made it out as if he was going further.

'I've got lots of other people to see, so I think I will pass, if you don't mind. If I keep going, I should make it to Westerham by sundown and I have some people to see there.'

Chapter 14

Taken greatly aback by his reluctance, the two friends reacted with great passion and begged him to stay.

'No, please don't go! We really want you to stay with us. We are so enjoying listening to you,' Angus pleaded.

It only took a moment for Felix to join in. 'Please, I beg you to stay for lunch, don't go on – there's plenty of time to share our food.'

'Very well,' the hiker gave in. 'I will stay and have some lunch.'

Deeply relieved, they began to unpack their lunches from their backpacks. The hiker took his pack off and got out some baguettes. The two men had much more: a wealth of food all carefully wrapped or in Tupperware containers: various slices of meat and fish, traditional pigs in blankets and pork pies, as well as a whole array of Christmas vegetables, sauces, desserts and cheeses. They placed them carefully on the plates.

'Let's have something to drink.' Angus pulled out a large bottle from his sack. 'This is a local white sparkling wine – we can't call it champagne, of course; it's produced at

Squerryes which is just a few miles to the west. Will you join us?'

The hiker shook his head and declined graciously. 'I'm teetotal for the time being, but thank you anyway. Would you like me to pray and bless the food?'

Both men nodded. The hiker closed his eyes and said simply, 'Father, we thank you for this food and for the gift of your Son, who became as we are so that we might become as he is. Forgive these brothers for their sins and help them to follow in the steps of Christ. Amen.'

Just as he finished praying, to their surprise, a phone in his pocket rang. He answered it, and then after a second or two, he turned away, cupping his hand over the phone and said, 'It's my Dad. I've got to take it. I won't be long, and I will be back.'

Just as he said that, Angus's bottle popped loudly of its own accord. The wine began to pour onto the ground, so Felix hurriedly grabbed the plastic wine glasses and thrust them under the bottle.

But when they turned round, the hiker had vanished.

'Where has he gone?' Angus's voice fluttered anxiously. 'I hope we didn't say something to offend him. I was so enjoying listening to him. Such an odd and mysterious person, though. Who was he and what was he up to?'

Both men looked around. Angus went into the woods, and Felix up to the path, but there was nothing and nobody to be seen. Just the wind blowing in the dead leaves.

Angus shook his head. 'How on earth did he just disappear?'

Suddenly, without warning, Felix fell to his knees and gasped so loudly Angus was alarmed.

'Oh, oh . . . I know who he was. How stupid I am. It was Jesus himself! Oh why, oh why didn't I recognise him? When he spoke to me and touched me, my heart was burning within me. I knew it was him, but I couldn't see him.'

Then he paused for a second, still on his knees, and then started laughing. 'Oh, you are such a complete idiot, Felix. It was Jesus and it's the road to Emmaus all over again.' His laughter turned to tears as he banged himself on the head, rolling around on the ground in a paroxysm of happiness.

'And all those signs I saw, like the strange frog and the tree and the leaves being blown, they were telling me he was coming.'

'Are you out of your mind? The road to Emmerdale? What on earth are you talking about?' Angus just stood there, bewildered.

'Not Emmerdale, you muppet. Emmaus. It's a story in the Bible, in Luke when Jesus appears to two of his disciples while they are walking to a village called Emmaus. They don't recognise him, but he rebukes them for their lack of faith and tells them all kinds of things they need to know. Then, at the end, when they implore him to stay with them, they start sharing a meal – and then, and only then, they recognise him. We've just reenacted the whole thing without even realising what we've done.'

Angus was intrigued. 'So, what you are saying is a story from the Bible just took place again and we were in it? And the hiker was Jesus?'

'Yes,' Felix said, standing up. 'That's exactly what I am saying.'

'Well, I'd like to look at the story, and he certainly was an unusual man, like nobody else I've ever met. I'm willing to have an open mind. But if it was him, why didn't he just say so? Why hide who he is?'

Felix shook his head. 'That's a very good question. In fact, you asked him exactly that question a few minutes ago. I'm not totally sure, but as far as I remember, what he said I think meant that what he wants is faith and faith is believing in what we can't see. We did see, but we were kept from recognizing him even though the answer was staring us in the face. If he just said, "I'm Jesus," that wouldn't be faith. It would be like the King in the story, simply overwhelming his bride.'

'So, what do we do now?' Angus asked.

'Well, in the story, if I recall rightly, they raced back to the other disciples. We need to find other Christians and tell them. So, let's go.'

'No,' Angus grimaced. 'What about the food? Are we just leaving it for the foxes?' He took another moment to think. 'I tell you what, forget the stupid Covid rules, let's pack it up quickly. For if it was Christ, then, after all, he's blessed it. Let's eat it at your house. It will be a lot warmer, and we can heat it up in the microwave.'

Quickly and eagerly, they packed up the food. Angus even managed to cork the wine with a little device he had in his back pocket.

'It might be a bit flat, but we can still enjoy it.'

Hurriedly they turned back towards Kemsing, skirting the wood and then turning left and southwards down the steep green hill, which Felix had recalled as being so recognisable from Emmetts.

As they were going down the hill, they noticed two figures toiling with difficulty up the hill, and as they drew near, they saw it was the two ladies, Jo and Vanessa, whom Felix had seen earlier.

'Happy Christmas again,' Felix called. 'You haven't seen a hiker with a big pack, have you?'

'You mean the young man who stopped to talk to us about a quarter of an hour ago?' Jo puffed, holding her sides. 'Yes, we did meet him and, in fact, now I think of it, he had a message for you. He said: "Tell my brothers they know where to find me." We didn't know who it was, because he didn't say anything else, just strode off. Good to know he's a friend of yours, who is he?'

Felix and Angus made them repeat the message word for word. Then Felix and Angus told them the whole story and explained. 'We think it was Jesus himself. But what does the message mean?'

'It was Jesus? Wow, if that is true, that's amazing,' Vanessa said, wide-eyed. 'Here in Kemsing? That will make the Sevenoaks Chronicle.' Then she thought for a moment. 'If it was him, well that's obvious what he means isn't it – he means a group of Christians, a church. That's where the disciples went after they had met Jesus, after all. Maybe, Felix, it's a message also that you need to stay. And if you did, everyone would be so happy. We all felt your sadness, but now you look like a man transformed.'

'Oh, Felix, everybody is so moved for you, and we do understand what you've been through, but we love you and would absolutely love it if you changed your mind,' Jo encouraged.

'I do feel like a completely different person,' Felix sighed, joy beneath his tone. 'I will have a think. Thank you so much for passing on that message. Let's have a full debrief tomorrow. I will try and collect my thoughts and maybe write up what happened. I'm so excited, but I don't exactly know what's happening to me.'

As they said goodbye to the ladies, who were excitedly talking to each other, they cut across the Pilgrims' Way and the fields in a direct line to the vicarage.

Angus was chewing things over. After a while, he said, 'I can see that for you this is life-changing and if it really was Christ – and I'm open-minded about that – that's unbelievable. But what about me? I'm not a religious person. I've never been to a church in my life. I wouldn't know what to do or what to say. He said, "tell my brothers", which was kind, not "tell my religious brother". Your job is to be religious. You can just go back to it, and your friends clearly want you back, but where does that leave me?'

By now, they stood at the door to Felix's house.

'Come in.' Felix fished his key from his coat pocket. 'I will warm up lunch, we can have a look at one of the gospels together and I can try and answer any questions you've got. The gospels are written for people just like you and me, people full of doubts and questions. But before I do anything, I have an email to write. And maybe . . . you should call your children?'